Thumbprint Mysteries

LETHAL DELIVERY, POSTAGE PREPAID

BY

KATHLEEN ANNE BARRETT

CB

CONTEMPORARY

a division of NTC/CONTEMPORARY PUBLISHING GROUP
Lincolnwood, Illinois USA

Thumbprint
Mysteries

YA
BAR

MORE THUMBPRINT MYSTERIES

by Kathleen Anne Barrett:

A Corpse in the Basement
Measure Once, Kill Twice

SW

This is a work of fiction. The characters, incidents, and dialogues are products of the author's imagination and are not to be construed as real. Any resemblance to actual events or persons, living or dead, is entirely coincidental.

Cover Illustration: Ellen Pettengell

ISBN: 0-8092-0645-5

Published by Contemporary Books,
a division of NTC/Contemporary Publishing Group, Inc.,
4255 West Touhy Avenue,
Lincolnwood (Chicago), Illinois 60646-1975 U.S.A.

90 QB 0 9 8 7 6 5 4 3 2 1

CHAPTER 1

Danny Patrinkis looked a little edgy and nervous the last time Dave and I saw him. We were at La Casa, one of our favorite Camden restaurants, and Danny was there with a woman neither of us had seen before.

"Hey, Danny, how are you doing?" Dave said when we spotted him. Danny jumped and looked around the room at the other customers.

"Hey, Dave, Annie. Fine, just fine." That was all he said. Then he looked down at his hands and played with his silverware.

Dave and I stood there for a few moments but Danny didn't look up again.

"Well, it was nice seeing you," Dave said.

Danny just nodded and kept looking at his fingers. He didn't introduce us to the woman, either.

"What the heck's the matter with him?" I said to Dave after we were seated at a table.

"I don't know," Dave said, "but he obviously has something on his mind."

That was over three months ago and I hadn't even thought about Danny again until the morning Dave gave me the news. "Did you hear about Danny Patrinkis?" he said as he pulled out one of my kitchen chairs.

I wrinkled my brow. "What do you mean?" I said.

"He was killed yesterday in a drive-by shooting. They think it was random. It was on the news. Didn't you see it?"

I stared at Dave as I shook my head. Dave and I had known Danny since we were freshmen in high school. We knew his whole family, in fact. We'd actually been pretty close at one time, so his death came as quite a shock to me even though we hadn't kept in touch over the years.

When Dave saw my face, he reached for my hand and told me to sit down. "Hey, I'm sorry," he said. "I didn't expect it to affect you so much. I guess I shouldn't have dumped it on you like that."

"No, I'm okay," I said. "It's just a little eerie, that's all. Seeing him like we did at La Casa after all those years and then having this happen to him so soon after we saw him. I just can't believe it's true."

"Yeah," Dave said in a sad voice. "I swear, if I ever find out who did this to him I'm going to . . ."

I put my hand on Dave's arm and he stopped talking. "I think this is one we should let the police take care of," I said. "We wouldn't have the slightest idea how to find someone like that. The guy probably didn't even have a reason. He probably didn't even know who Danny was."

Dave looked down at the table and tightened his jaw.

A few moments later, he let out a big sigh and looked up at me. "You're right," he said with a defeated sound to his voice. "I guess we should leave it to the police."

I probably don't have to tell you how long *that* plan lasted. I'm Annie Johnson, by the way. I live in Camden, New Jersey, and so does Dave Barrio. We've been here all our lives. We're both thirty-four years old and we went to high school together, spending most of our days on the street instead of in school where we were supposed to be. When we turned sixteen, we dropped out and made our hanging out official. We had a good time for a while until Dave's dad died, and he had to go to work to help support his mom and his little sister. He couldn't get a job without a degree so he just did odd jobs for people, making things and repairing anything that needed it. Then one day he started his own carpentry business and has turned himself into a real success. He has two guys working for him fulltime and he's an artist at his craft. You should see some of the things he's done. People hire him from all over the place and pay him pretty big bucks.

I was sent to live with my aunt when I was ten because my mom couldn't take care of me. I never met my dad, but I think he's the one who started my mother drinking. She had no job, no money, and no education when she had me, and then he just dumped her without any warning. Maybe that's why I've never gotten married. I'm probably afraid I'll end up with someone like my dad and spend the rest of my life regretting it.

I swore I'd never grow up to be like my mom but I guess I sort of did anyway (except for getting pregnant, that is). By the time I turned twenty, I was a hopeless alcoholic just like she was. I was still living with my aunt but I hardly ever came home. I spent all my time with other alcoholics, which just seemed to make the problem worse. It was like no one wanted anyone else to quit drinking because then you'd lose one of your drinking buddies. And it also sort of made you look bad in comparison when someone else was on the wagon.

I was one of the lucky ones, though, because I had Dave. One night when I felt like I was really losing it, I went to see him. The next day he took me to an AA meeting and he dragged me there, day after day, until I was finally willing to go by myself. It took me over a year before I stopped wanting a drink and another five or six before I stopped being afraid I'd start again. Even now, fifteen years later, a trace of the fear is still there. Dave says it's a good fear though, a fear that keeps me sober.

Two years and seven months after my first AA meeting, I got my GED. Then I started making crafts, just little things made of wood with something painted on them. I'm no artist so I use stencils most of the time, but I work really hard at it and I take pride in what I do. If something doesn't come out right the first time, I paint over it and do it again until I'm satisfied. Today, I sell at flea markets and craft fairs all over New Jersey and Pennsylvania, and I make things to order for three different stores in the area. I make a decent living and I own my own house in one of my favorite sections of Camden.

Last year, I was falsely accused of murder and Dave and I solved the case since no one but us seemed to have any interest in doing so. Then a short time later, a friend of Dave's was murdered and we solved that case too, so I guess it was only natural that we'd get ourselves involved in the investigation of Danny Patrinkis's death after all. It's not that we don't think the police can do a good job, but we know from past experience that sometimes Dave and I can do better.

It was when we talked to Mrs. Patrinkis at Danny's viewing that we decided to go back on our decision to stay out of it. Danny's mother was in her early eighties, needed a walker to get around, and looked as if she was in a great deal of pain every time she moved. We'd met her many times before, of course, but it had been close to twenty years since either of us had seen her. It took us a minute or two to get her to remember us.

"Mrs. Patrinkis," Dave said in a warm voice when we came in. Mrs. Patrinkis was sitting on a metal chair near the entrance to the viewing room and a young woman was standing at her side. Dave took Mrs. Patrinkis's hands in his and gave her a kind smile. "I'm Dave Barrio," he said, "and this is Annie Johnson. I don't know if you remember us. It's been a long time."

Mrs. Patrinkis squinted at Dave and then at me. Then a faint smile slowly crossed her face. "Dave and Annie," she said in a welcoming voice. "Of course I remember you. I only wish Danny could be here to see you."

"We saw him a few months ago, Mrs. Patrinkis," I said. "It was so good to see him."

She smiled at that and squeezed the back of my hand. Then she made an attempt to turn toward the young woman beside her, but she couldn't move her head more than an inch. She tried to move her whole body instead but that appeared to be even harder, so she finally gave up and moved her hand in the woman's direction.

"I want you to meet Donna," she said. "Danny's wife."

I'm quite sure my surprise showed on my face but Donna didn't seem to notice. She smiled weakly and held out her hand to me and then to Dave. "Hello," she said in a small voice. "It's nice to meet you."

I smiled and said something I hoped was appropriate.

We spent a few more minutes with them and then walked around the room. We saw quite a few people we knew, including Danny's brother Jim who is a year older than we are. Jim approached us and shook both our hands. Jim is at least six-four with an extremely muscular weight lifter's body—just like Danny's had been—but he has dark hair and Danny's had been red.

"How have you guys been?" Jim said in his deep voice. "I read about you in the paper a few months back. Was that for real? Did you really solve those murders?"

Dave and I both laughed. "We sure did," Dave said.

Jim had a funny look on his face, like he wanted to say something but he wasn't sure how to phrase it. "Are you guys private detectives or what?" he asked.

We explained that we weren't and told him how we had gotten involved in the murder investigations and eventually moved on to another topic. When I asked Jim what he was doing now, he got an uncomfortable look on his face. It lasted only a moment but it was definitely there.

"I'm a car mechanic," he said as he carefully watched our faces. "Same as always."

"Where's Bonnie?" I said then. Bonnie was Danny's younger sister. I think she was only about seven or eight when we started high school.

Jim looked around the room until he spotted her. "There she is," he said, and he pointed to a group of women near the center of the room.

I knew which one was Bonnie right away. She towered above the rest of them and her hair was a deep red, something like Danny's only quite a bit darker. We said good-bye to Jim and walked toward her.

"Did you notice how uptight he was?" I whispered to Dave after we were far enough away from Jim that I was certain he wouldn't hear us.

Dave gave me a little smile. "Yeah, I did," he whispered

back. "I wonder what that was all about."

When we reached Bonnie, Dave touched her shoulder. "Hi, Bonnie," he said. "You probably don't remember us but we were good friends of Danny's in high school. I'm Dave Barrio and this is Annie Johnson."

Bonnie smiled politely at both of us. "Hi," she said. "Thanks for coming. I'm sure Danny would have appreciated it."

We talked a little more (she clearly didn't remember us) and then moved on. We saw a lot of people we hadn't seen in nearly twenty years. Sometimes we recognized them but usually they recognized us. Maybe it was because we were together. It was quite a reunion, as funerals often are. It's such a strange feeling. I'd catch myself having a good time and then I'd feel guilty when I'd remember why I was there.

When we were ready to leave, we looked for Mrs. Patrinkis so we could say good-bye. She was sitting near the casket with Bonnie at her side. There was no one else within hearing distance. When we approached, Mrs. Patrinkis looked a bit anxious and excited. I asked her if she was all right and she said that she was fine, but she told Bonnie that she was cold and asked her to get her her wrap. Then she waited until Bonnie was out of earshot and whispered something to me and Dave.

Both of us stared at her with our mouths open. I looked around to make sure no one had heard her and I was pretty sure that no one had.

"Come to the house early, the morning after the funeral," she said in an urgent voice. "When you see the letters, you will know that I am right."

CHAPTER 2

We were silent for the first few minutes of our ride home, both thinking about what Mrs. Patrinkis had told us and what it might mean.

"So does this mean we're going to start poking around into Danny's murder?" Dave finally said. I couldn't tell by his voice whether he wanted to or not.

"I don't know," I said. "What do you think?"

"Well, it sounds kind of interesting," he said calmly, "but maybe we should hold off deciding until we've taken a look at those letters. Mrs. Patrinkis might be reading more into them than there is. There might be nothing to them at all."

"Uh-huh," I said and tried to hide my smile. He was totally hooked already. I could tell.

"Do you remember the woman who was with Danny when we saw him at La Casa?" I said.

Dave wrinkled his brow. "No, not really," he said. "And that reminds me. I didn't know he was married, did you?"

"No, I didn't," I said, "and the woman at La Casa wasn't Donna."

Dave turned and looked at me with one eyebrow arched.

The funeral the next morning was even better attended than the viewing. I looked around for the woman we'd seen at La Casa with Danny, but I couldn't find her.

"You look like an untrained detective," Dave whispered in my ear. "Who are you looking for?"

"That woman Danny was with," I said. "I just thought she might be here."

Dave gave me an amused but affectionate smile.

Now that Dave and I had pretty much decided to try to solve Danny's murder, I had an almost unbearable urge to go up to everyone at the funeral and ask them if they had any idea who did it. I thought about talking to Jim and Bonnie, maybe just to let them know we'd be in touch, but I decided it would be better to wait until we'd seen the letters. Dave could be right after all. There really might not be anything to them.

The next day, Dave picked me up at 8:15 A.M. and we drove to Mrs. Patrinkis's house. She'd asked us to come early, so we decided that getting there a little before nine would probably be acceptable. I was so excited about seeing the mysterious letters that I couldn't stop fidgeting. I had barely slept four hours the night before, wondering what could possibly be in them and who they might be from. I wished she at least had given us a little hint, but I don't think she felt safe talking about them at the funeral home.

At 8:45, Dave and I knocked on Mrs. Patrinkis's door. When she hadn't answered after three or four hard knocks, I rang the bell. Mrs. Patrinkis lived in one of the medium-poor sections of town where most of the houses still have their windows. The streets are strewn with trash, however, and they're not at all safe at night.

"Did you get the impression that Mrs. Patrinkis was hard of hearing when we saw her at the viewing?" I asked Dave after a few more minutes had passed.

"I don't know," he said. "We were so close to her when we were talking that I didn't notice."

I gave Dave an anxious look and he gave me a similar one back. "Let's go and look through the windows," I said.

We stepped off the small concrete stoop and peered through a tiny, grimy window to the right of the front door. I could barely see through it and what I could see looked pretty normal to me. I was about to try the window to the left when I saw something move. It was Mrs. Patrinkis, walking as slowly as a snail toward the door and stopping to rest against her walker after every step. I felt a mixture of guilt and pity that brought tears to my eyes. When Dave saw her, he winced and put his arm around me. It was at least two minutes more before she reached the door.

"Dave, Annie," Mrs. Patrinkis said in a nearly breathless voice. "Please—come in—sit down—in the living room." She was taking large breaths between every few words and her face was pinched with pain.

"Wait," I said. "I'll bring some chairs from the kitchen and we can sit right here."

Dave smiled at me. "I'll get them," he said. "You two stay here."

When Dave returned, he was carrying three aluminum

chairs with yellow plastic seats. He placed them near the door and helped Mrs. Patrinkis sit down. Then we waited for what must have been five minutes until her breathing was back to normal.

"Can we get you anything?" I asked her after she appeared to have her strength back.

"No, dear, I'll be all right now. This is what I needed, to get off my feet."

Dave and I smiled at her and then exchanged uncomfortable looks.

"Mrs. Patrinkis," I said, "you mentioned something about some letters you wanted to show us. Can you tell us what they said?"

Mrs. Patrinkis closed her eyes and took a deep breath. "I want you to read them for yourselves," she said. "It is better you read them yourselves."

"But you really believe they prove what you suspect?" Dave said.

"Yes, I do," she said. "You will agree when you have read them. You will see that I am right."

Dave nodded. "Okay, where are they?" he said.

"They're in his room," Mrs. Patrinkis said. "You will have to go and get them."

We both frowned. "You mean they're not here?" I said.

She looked a bit puzzled. "Yes, of course they are here. They are in his room. It's the first room to the left at the top of the stairs."

"You mean he was living here with you?" Dave asked her.

Mrs. Patrinkis smiled. "Yes," she said and then her smile faded. "Danny was such a good boy. He took care of me. Now there is no one left."

"But what about Jim?" I said. "He lives nearby, doesn't he? And what about Bonnie?"

Mrs. Patrinkis stiffened. "Bonnie has five little ones," she said. "She has no time for anything else. She is too busy."

"But what about Jim?" Dave said. "He could help you."

Mrs. Patrinkis didn't even respond to Dave's question. "The letters are in a box in the corner of the room," she said in a tight voice. "You may bring them down with you."

When Dave and I had entered Danny's room, I whispered, "What do you think that was all about? Do you think she had some sort of falling out with Jim and Bonnie?"

"It sure sounds like it, at least with Jim," he whispered back. "Come to think of it, I didn't see them together at either the funeral or the viewing. We'll have to ask him about it. But Bonnie was with her when we went to say good-bye, and five kids would take a lot of work. She probably doesn't have any extra time and we don't even know where she lives. She might not be that close."

"Well, at least she's on good terms with Donna," I said.

Dave nodded but then he frowned. "Yes, but look at this room. Do you get the impression that a man and a woman were living here, or just a man?"

I looked around. The room was small and cluttered with one twin-sized bed shoved against a wall. There were sneakers and dirty socks on the floor, the bed was unmade, and three loaded ashtrays were on the nightstand and dresser. I opened the closet door. No women's clothing, just a few denim shirts, two pairs of jeans in a heap on the floor, and three newly dry-cleaned pale green uniforms with the emblem of a package delivery service sewn on the upper left sleeves.

"You're right," I said. "It looks like he was living here

alone unless Donna was in another room."

Dave gave me a look. "In another room?" he said. "What for?"

I shrugged and secretly agreed with him but my curiosity was aroused. "I'm going to take a little look around," I whispered.

Dave rolled his eyes at me. "Okay," he said, "but make it quick and try to keep quiet."

I sighed and went into the next room. It was a bathroom, also very tiny. The floor was covered with a bright blue shag carpet that couldn't have been cleaned in many months. The blue and green striped wallpaper was peeling in at least five different places and the part nearest the tub was water-stained. There was a shaver on the sink along with a half-used tube of toothpaste, a worn-out toothbrush, and a dirty bar of soap. On the top of the toilet tank was a can of shaving cream and a bottle of cologne. The sink, toilet, and tub were covered with grime and the room smelled so bad that I opened the window to let in some air.

The next room was a bedroom, much larger than the first and far neater. The curtains were sheer and white with wide ruffles at the edges. The wallpaper had large pink roses against a cream background. There were lace doilies on the mahogany dressers and nightstands and on the arms and back of an overstuffed chair. The chair was upholstered in a tiny rose print that went very well with the wallpaper. A large crucifix hung above the bed, which was covered with a cream, chenille bedspread, and pictures with religious-type scenes nearly covered the walls.

There was a bathroom adjoining the bedroom, also surprisingly neat and clean, with pink and cream towels and rose-print porcelain soap dishes.

I went back to Danny's room and found Dave

rummaging through a desk.

"What are you doing?" I said. "Did you find the letters?"

"Not yet," he said. "I figured we might as well search the whole room while we have the chance. Did you find anything?"

"No," I said. "But someone's obviously been cleaning house for Mrs. Patrinkis and not for Danny. Her bedroom and bathroom are spotless. She never could have done it herself."

"Well, no one's touched this place in years from the looks of it," Dave said.

"I wonder if he asked them not to," I said.

"I was wondering the same thing myself," Dave said. "Look at this."

Dave handed me a file with a Philadelphia city map and three others for nearby suburbs. On all four maps, a large number of the streets were highlighted in yellow.

I frowned and looked at Dave. "What do you think this means?" I said.

"I don't know," Dave said, "but I'd like to take it with us. Do you think you can fit it in your bag?"

I tilted my head sideways. "What, are you kidding?" I said. "I could fit the Empire State Building in this thing."

Dave laughed as I folded the file in half and neatly placed it in my purse. Then he walked to the closet and looked at the uniforms. "I wonder what he did for them," he said.

"I think those are the uniforms they wear to deliver packages," I said. "That's what I always see them in. He probably drove a truck on a route and delivered packages."

Dave laughed. "You ought to know," he said. "You order more things from catalogs than any ten people I know."

"Very funny," I said, but Dave wasn't listening. He was staring into a sack he'd found on a shelf above the uniforms.

He whistled. "Come and take a look at this," he said.

I walked over to the closet and peered into the bag. It was filled with money, all fifties and hundreds from what I could see.

"I hope you're not going to ask me to put *that* in my purse," I said.

Dave laughed but it was a nervous laugh, and he quickly put the sack back where he'd found it.

"No," he said. "The last thing we need is to be implicated in whatever Danny was involved in. I'm going to tell the cops about this and let them pick it up themselves."

"You mean you think he was involved in something illegal?" I said.

"Why else would he be keeping his money in a sack? I doubt he was afraid of banks. I also doubt he was hiding his huge income from delivering packages from the IRS. It had to be more than that."

"Yeah, you're probably right," I said. "Did you finish searching the desk?"

"Nothing in there but the maps," he said.

It was then that I opened the shoebox. "Oh, my gosh," I said. "I think I found the letters."

CHAPTER 3

"Let's read them before we bring them downstairs," I said.

"Why?" Dave said. "What difference does it make? She's already seen them. She knows what they say."

"I know, but we don't, and I'd like to get our first look at them without her being able to see our reaction."

"Well, okay, but hang on," he said. "I'm going to check on her. She's awful quiet down there. I don't want her sneaking up on us."

"She's not going to sneak up on us," I said. "You saw her. She can barely move. And if she sees you, she'll tell us to come down."

"I won't let her see me," Dave said. "Don't get so worked up. I just want to make sure she's all right."

I gave him one of my frustrated looks and held my breath. When he came back, he had a little smile on his face. "She's sound asleep," he said. "She'll never know how long we were up here."

I let out a deep breath and opened the first envelope. The envelope had Danny's name on it in letters cut out from a magazine. There was no address and no postmark. I took out the single sheet of paper. Dave stepped behind me and looked over my shoulder as I read it.

"I see what she means," he said.

"Yeah, me too."

The letter was very short but the meaning was pretty clear. It said: "IF yOu dO NoT Stay oUt of mATters wHIch arE NOnE oF YOUR BusiNESS, yoU wiLL BE VerY SORRy."

There were four more very much like it. Since none of them were dated, we couldn't be sure which order they'd been sent in.

The second one in the pile said: "SOmeONE you Care For May get HURT if You do noT MinD youR BUSiNess."

The third one said: "ThaT SomEone MAY be You."

The fourth one said: "YoU HAVe BEEn WARned."

And the fifth one said: "YoU WENt TOO fAR aND MusT PaY TO saVE yOUR LifE."

None of them were signed, of course, but all five of them had Danny's name on the envelope.

"I wish we knew what they were talking about," I said. "There isn't even a clue in any of them about what it is they wanted him to stay out of. I'll bet they got him asking for money, though. I wish we knew when they'd come."

"Come on. Let's see if Mrs. Patrinkis has any ideas. He may have talked to her about it. How else would she know about the letters?"

I frowned. "But why would he want to worry her like that? I'd think she'd be the last person he would tell."

Dave looked at me for a moment. "You know, you're right," he said. "And if someone else told her about them, why would they do it?"

We took the letters downstairs and gently woke up Mrs. Patrinkis. We pretended not to have read them yet and went through them again, acting shocked and horrified as we did so.

"How did you find out about the letters?" I asked her after we were through. "Did Danny show them to you?"

Her eyes filled with tears. "No, Danny wouldn't have wanted to worry me. He didn't say a word about them. He never would have told me."

"Then who told you, Mrs. Patrinkis?"

"It was Donna," she said. "Donna came here one day when Danny was at work and she told me. When I didn't believe her, she went upstairs and found the letters and showed them to me."

"Didn't she live here with you and Danny?" I asked.

"No," Mrs. Patrinkis said. "She did not live with us. Danny said it was because of the cats. She couldn't live with the cats."

I was confused but I wasn't sure what to say. I hadn't seen any cats anywhere but I was afraid that if I pointed that out, Mrs. Patrinkis might get worried. I couldn't imagine her taking care of them by herself.

"How many cats do you have?" Dave said, relieving me of my problem.

Mrs. Patrinkis sighed. "I had four cats," she said, "but they're all gone now. The health department took them away."

"Oh, I'm so sorry, Mrs. Patrinkis," I said. "How did the

health department find out about them?"

"I don't know," she said with a sad look. "They just came one day and took them away."

I squeezed her hand and frowned at Dave.

"When did Danny move in with you?" Dave asked.

Mrs. Patrinkis put a thoughtful expression on her face as if she were trying to remember. "It was a long time ago," she said. "Before Christmas. Or maybe Thanksgiving."

"So it was almost a year?" I said.

She wrinkled her brow and said, "Before Thanksgiving."

"Were Danny and Donna getting divorced?" I said. "Is that why he moved away from her?"

"Oh," Mrs. Patrinkis said, as if in some sort of distress. "No, I don't think so. Oh, dear, I hope not. They're such a nice couple."

Dave and I exchanged looks.

"Mrs. Patrinkis, what did Donna say about the letters? Did she tell you how she knew about them in the first place?" I asked.

"She said Danny told her that he was in trouble and that he needed money. She wanted me to give it to him. When I told her I didn't have any, she went upstairs and brought down the letters."

"How long was she upstairs before she came back down again? Do you remember that?" I asked.

"A very short time," Mrs. Patrinkis said. "Just like you."

I sighed. "What did she say when she showed them to you?"

"She told me I had to give Danny the money or they would hurt him."

"Why was she so sure you had any money?" I asked. "Did Danny tell her that?"

"A long time ago, after he and Donna got married, Danny would come to me when they needed help. But that was only small amounts, never anything big. I had money saved from when Danny's papa died, but it's all gone now. It was all used up years ago. Danny knew that."

"Did you explain that to Donna?" Dave said.

"I tried," Mrs. Patrinkis said, "but she was too angry to listen."

"Did she say how much he asked her for? Did she tell you if he asked her for a certain amount?"

"No, she just said he needed money. She didn't know how much."

I nodded and gave her a comforting look. "Did Donna know anything else about the letters?" I asked. "Did she know what they were talking about? Did she have any idea what they wanted Danny to stay out of?"

"No. She only knew that Danny was in trouble and that he needed money. I think she was afraid for both of them."

"Why was she afraid for herself?" I said.

"I don't know," Mrs. Patrinkis said. "She just said she was afraid."

Dave took hold of Mrs. Patrinkis's hands. "Mrs. Patrinkis," he said, "I know it may be hard for you to remember this, but can you tell us when Donna came to the house and showed you the letters?"

Mrs. Patrinkis looked as if she were thinking, but then her expression changed to an anxious one. "I can't remember," she said in an agitated voice.

"It's all right," Dave said. "Don't worry. We can always ask Donna."

I already knew the answer to the next question I asked, but I wanted to see what Mrs. Patrinkis would say.

"Mrs. Patrinkis, was Danny ever in any kind of trouble that you know of, even as a boy, I mean?"

Mrs. Patrinkis stiffened slightly and raised her head a bit. "Danny was a good boy," she said. "He never got in any trouble that was his fault. He hung around with no-good troublemakers. It was their fault Danny got in trouble."

"Was this when he was a kid?" Dave said. "Are you talking about when he was in high school?"

She hesitated just a moment and then said "Yes" in a tight voice.

"How about later?" Dave asked in a gentle voice. "Had he been hanging around with anyone lately who got him into trouble?"

Mrs. Patrinkis breathed in and out a few times. "I didn't know about them," she said. "I don't know who they are."

"But you think there was someone?" I said.

"Who else could send such letters?" she said in a teary voice. "Who else could have killed him?"

"Did *Danny* ever ask you for money?" Dave said. "I mean recently, like in the last several months or so?"

"Not after my money was gone," Mrs. Patrinkis said. "Danny always helped *me* after that."

"Did you ever get the impression that Danny had a lot of extra money?" I said. "Before Donna asked you to give him money, I mean."

"Extra?" she said with a puzzled look. "No, I certainly never got that impression."

"But he always had money when you needed it?"

"Danny always took very good care of me," she said. "Whenever I needed something, he always helped."

We talked awhile longer and then said good-bye to

Mrs. Patrinkis. I promised her that I'd come to visit from time to time.

"You don't think Danny could've gotten himself involved in something just to make extra money for his mother, do you?" I asked Dave when we reached the car.

"I was wondering the same thing myself," he said. "If she's right, and I'm sure she is, he cared about her a lot. I can remember him in high school getting really upset one time because she was sick. He was totally bent out of shape."

I sighed. "God, I hope he didn't go and get himself killed just because he was trying to do a good deed."

"Why does it matter?" Dave said. "He's dead either way."

"I know," I said, "but somehow it seems worse if he died doing something good. If he died doing something bad, you can at least say he brought it on himself."

Dave stared at me with his mouth open. "But he was murdered, Annie. How can you say he brought that on himself?"

Now I was starting to get annoyed. That isn't what I meant and it bothered me that he didn't understand. "I didn't mean that," I said. "All I meant was that it's all that much worse if he was totally innocent." I looked at Dave's face and he still didn't seem to understand. "Let's drop it," I said. "I have a long day planned for tomorrow. I want to talk to Donna about those letters. I'd like to find out how she really knew about them. Want to come along?"

Now Dave gave me a big grin. "You bet I do," he said. "We're a detecting team, don't forget."

I gave him a warm smile and was once again surprised at how relieved I was that there was no longer any tension between us. I really care far more than I like to admit.

CHAPTER 4

I got up at 5:30 the next morning so I could get in close to a full day's work before I went to see Donna. I'd learned from Mrs. Patrinkis that Donna worked as a city bus driver and that she started work at noon. We could catch the bus in Williamstown and ride with her to the Deptford Mall. Dave and I had agreed the night before to meet at my house at 10:45. That would give us plenty of time to meet her bus and we could always wait in the car if we were early.

I had a larger breakfast than usual (three scrambled eggs with onions and green peppers, and two pieces of toast), cleaned up the kitchen, and then spent half an hour finishing a birdhouse I'd been working on. I used up another hour on a custom sign that someone had ordered and an hour or so designing plaques for a baby's room. I love working in the early morning hours. I feel like the rest of the world is asleep and I'm being let in on all the secrets of what goes on before they get up. By 9:30, of course, the feeling was gone and I was hungry again. I made myself some rye toast and a pot of coffee and went back to work. I finished designing two of the plaques and was working on a third when Dave came to the door. I was amazed when I looked at my watch. I couldn't believe I'd gotten that much work done, and I still had most of the day ahead of me. It was a very satisfying feeling.

We took I-76 to Route 42, got on the Atlantic City expressway and then off again at the first exit. The Park-and-Ride lot, where people can leave their cars and ride the bus to work, was only a block or so down from the exit on Sicklerville Road. It was only 11:45 when we arrived so we had to wait fifteen minutes for the bus. We spent most of the time talking about what we planned to say to Donna and how we should handle it. She was bound to be a little upset at our questioning her while she was working. In fact, she might even turn us down. Worse yet, we wouldn't be alone and she might not feel free to talk. There were at least a dozen people waiting at the stop and more pulling into the parking lot every minute.

"Maybe this wasn't such a good idea after all," I said to Dave. "I really don't want her to hold anything back or feel like she can't talk because there are other people around. And she might appreciate it if we asked her first instead of just pouncing on her like this."

"So what are you saying?" Dave asked with a hint of annoyance in his voice.

"Well, maybe we should get on the bus like we planned, but we could just ask her if we can arrange to meet with her some other time. That way she won't feel so pressured and cornered."

"I'm not riding that bus all the way to the mall for nothing," Dave said. "Either we talk to her now or we're leaving."

I took a breath. "We don't have to ride the bus," I said calmly. "We can ask her when she pulls up and we don't even have to get on."

"And what if she says no?"

"Then we're no worse off than we would've been if we'd gotten on the bus. She's either willing to talk to us or she's not."

Dave stared out the side window and didn't answer for a few moments. "All right," he finally said. "Let's try to make it for tonight, though. I'm going to have to work all day tomorrow."

As it turned out, all of our worries were for nothing. "I'd be glad to talk to you," Donna said as soon as I brought up the subject, "but I can't do it now. I'm not allowed to talk to any of the passengers while I'm driving." She gave me an apologetic smile and pointed to a sign near the driver's seat.

"That's perfectly all right," I said. "We were just hoping to make an appointment with you. I know this isn't much notice, but would it be possible for you to do it tonight? Dave really wants to be there and tonight's the only time that's good for him."

Donna thought for a moment and said, "Sure. Stop by my place anytime between seven and eight." Then she gave me the address.

Dave was sort of quiet on the way home and I was afraid he was angry with me. "Are you upset about something?" I said.

"No, I'm fine. Everything's fine." His voice was tense and unfriendly.

"Are you sure?" I said. "You sound like there's something wrong. If there is, I wish you'd tell me."

He tightened his grip on the steering wheel. "Do you

always have to be in control of everything?" he said. "I said there's nothing wrong. If I wanted to talk to you about something, I'd be doing it."

I sighed and gave up. I hate it when he gets like that. I feel so helpless. We have been good friends since we were fifteen years old, and then a few months ago we started having a romantic relationship. Now everything's a disaster. I can't talk to him like I used to, and I feel uncomfortable whenever he's in a funny mood, which is almost all of the time lately. I don't know what's wrong with him and he won't tell me. I've even asked him if he wants to go back to being just friends, but that only makes him more upset. I really don't know what to do. I didn't say a word the rest of the way home. I figured it was the safest approach.

"Do you want to pick me up again tonight?" I said when we got to my house.

"Yeah. I'll see you at seven."

"Okay," I said, hoping he'd look at me. When he didn't, I got out of the car and said good-bye. He didn't say anything back, so I closed the door and went inside. Then I spent the next half-hour crying and the one after that eating. I had this really strange urge to call my mom, but I hadn't talked to her in over fifteen years, so I didn't think that would do me any good. It wouldn't have done any good even if I'd talked to her yesterday, for that matter. She never did have any interest in my life.

I puttered around the house for a while, picking things up and doing a little cleaning. I even rearranged some of my furniture. I figured all that work entitled me to a nap. I was really using that as an excuse, of course. The real reason for the nap was to drown out how I was feeling about Dave. I just wanted to turn everything off for a while. I set my alarm for 6:30 and fell sound asleep.

When my alarm went off, I felt awful. I was groggy and achy and I wanted to stay in bed. I knew I couldn't, though. Dave was upset enough already. All I needed was to tell him I'd changed my mind about going. I washed my face with cold water, put on some makeup, and went downstairs to have a cup of tea. I was rinsing my cup when Dave came to the door, ten minutes early.

When I opened it, he put his arms around me and buried his face in my hair. "I'm sorry," he whispered. "I'm so sorry. I don't know why I get that way sometimes. I know I'm hurting you but I just can't seem to stop. I don't even know where it comes from. It's like something just takes ahold of me and I start saying things I don't really mean. I'm not used to this kind of relationship, you know. This is a very hard thing for me to do. When we were friends, I always wanted it to be more, but now that it is, I don't know how to handle it sometimes."

I did my best to wipe the rush of tears from my eyes. "It's all right," I said. "It's okay."

It really isn't all right, of course, but I say that every time. I don't know why. I guess I just don't know what else to say. And I think I'm also afraid that if I give him a hard time about the way he treats me, I'll lose him.

"No, it isn't all right," he said. "But I hope you'll forgive me. I'll try harder. I promise."

I smiled at him and touched his cheek. "I do forgive you," I said. "You know I do. Come on, let's go."

The drive to Donna's apartment was slightly tense but a whole lot more pleasant than the one we'd had from the bus stop that morning. Donna lived in an apartment building not far from my house on Thirty-eighth Street. It was old and run-down with a broken security lock on the barred front door. We walked up two flights of stairs to the third floor and knocked on her door. She answered immediately, wearing a deep gold sweater and matching jeans. Donna looked to be in her late twenties, maybe five to eight years younger than Danny. She was about five-six with a good figure and medium-length red hair. Her skin was very pale and she had tiny brown freckles on her slightly upturned nose. She was pretty cute, to tell you the truth.

"Hi, come on in," she said in a friendly voice. She had an open beer in her hand and offered one to us. We both said no.

"Suit yourself," she said.

She motioned toward the couch and asked us to sit down. The room was cluttered with magazines, empty beer and soda cans, and food wrappers. Half of a Twinkie lay on the coffee table and two cigarette butts floated in an almost empty cup of coffee.

"What can I do for you?" she said. She seemed good-natured enough. The mess didn't appear to bother her at all, so I tried not to let it bother me. It was surprising, though. I never would have guessed by her personal appearance that she would keep her house looking like that.

"We wanted to ask you a few questions about Danny," Dave said.

"Shoot," she said. "I got nothing to hide."

I smiled at her. I liked her easy manner and her friendliness. "How did you know about those letters that were sent to Danny?" I asked. "The threatening ones cut out of magazines."

"Danny showed them to me," she said. "He was real scared, let me tell you. He wanted money from me but I told him to get lost. He never did nothing for me and I wasn't about to do anything for him." Her relaxed expression had changed to a bitter one when she answered my question. There was bitterness in her voice as well.

"So you really didn't get along with him at all?" I asked.

Donna changed positions in her chair. "No, I didn't say that. We got along just fine. I loved Danny, I really did. We were going to get back together. We were just trying to work things out. You know how it is."

I nodded and tried to look like I believed her. "I'm really sorry things worked out the way they did for you," I said. "Did you have any idea when were you going to get back together?"

"Not till his old lady died, I'll tell you that," she said. "That's why we split up in the first place. He was going to have her come live with us and I said no way, man. There ain't no way I'm going to live with that woman. So what does he do? He up and moves out on me and moves in with her. Can you beat that? He chooses his old lady over his wife, and then he has the nerve to come asking me for money."

You may find this hard to believe, but I was at a loss for words. Luckily, Dave wasn't. "When he showed you the letters, did he tell you what they were about?" Dave said. "Did he have any idea who was threatening him or what they wanted him to stay out of?"

"If he did, he didn't tell me," Donna said.

"But he gave you the impression he had no money of his own?" I said.

"All I know is he asked me to give him as much as I could spare. I told him to go ask his mama."

"When did he come to see you?" Dave said.

"It couldn't have been more than a week before he died," Donna said.

"Do you know if he was involved in anything illegal?" Dave said.

When Donna gave him a cagey look, Dave said, "You don't have to protect him now, you know. We're just trying to find out who killed him, and the more we know the better we'll be able to do that."

She looked at both of us and sighed. "Yeah, I believe he was. But if you want the details, you'll have to ask Jimmy. He knows a lot more about that than I could ever tell you."

Dave and I looked at each other. "Do you think there's any possibility that his death could be related to that?"

Donna shrugged. "Sure, I guess. From what I heard, these guys aren't the sort you want to mess with. But like I told you, you'd better ask Jimmy. Danny wouldn't tell me nothing about that business. He just told me to stay out of it. He said it was safer that way. The less I knew the better."

"When did he say that?" I asked with a frown.

"I don't know," Donna said. "He said it every time I brought it up. He was always acting so strange, like he was afraid of something. I figured it had something to do with that, so I asked him about it but he'd never tell me. Just told me to keep my nose out of places it didn't belong or I might lose it someday."

I raised my eyebrows.

"Well, I don't think he meant it literally," Donna said.

I wasn't so sure.

CHAPTER 5

That night I tried reaching Danny's brother Jim, but he wasn't home and he didn't have an answering machine. I called Donna and asked her if she could give me his work phone number. She sounded a little hesitant.

"I'm not sure he'd want you calling him at work," she said. "He might get in trouble for that."

After I explained that I couldn't reach him at home, she gave in. I was a little surprised that she'd hesitated at all since she was the one who had suggested that we talk to Jim in the first place.

The next morning I tried Jim's home number again, got no answer, and called him at work.

"Jimmy's not working today," said a man with a gruff voice. "It's his day off."

"Do you know where I can reach him?" I said.

"How should I know, lady?" he said. "Try him at home."

I sighed. "Does he work tomorrow?" I asked.

I heard some rustling of paper. "Yeah, he's here tomorrow. Seven to seven." He hung up without saying good-bye.

I was disappointed. I was really counting on at least making some arrangements to see him, and now I'd probably have to wait another twenty-four hours. Well, I'd just have to forget about him for the time being and focus on somebody else. I'd already talked to Mrs. Patrinkis and Donna, but I hadn't talked to Bonnie. I didn't have her number either so I decided I'd have to call Donna again. It was better than bothering poor Mrs. Patrinkis.

This time Donna sounded annoyed, but she did give me the number. "Now in case you don't reach her at home, I don't know her work phone number, so don't bother calling me back to ask me," she said.

I made a face I was glad she couldn't see. "Do you know where she works even if you don't know the number?" I said in a sweet voice.

"She works at the post office," Donna said, "but I don't think she can take personal calls."

"The Camden post office?" I asked.

"That's the one," Donna said. "You have any more numbers you want?"

She was really starting to get on my nerves. I wanted to be careful, though. I didn't want to get on her bad side in case I needed more information from her at a later time.

"Not for now," I said in a cheerful voice. "Thanks, Donna."

It was only 8:30 A.M. so there was still a chance I'd catch Bonnie before she left for work. I dialed her number and got her answering machine. I was in the process of leaving a message when she picked up. I reminded her of who I was and told her why I wanted to talk with her.

"But it was just a random shooting," she said in a voice full of concern. "If that's what the police think, why should you think any different?"

I told her about the letters her mother had shown me, and then I told her about my conversation with Donna.

"Donna doesn't know what she's talking about," Bonnie said. "She's always shooting her mouth off about something. Danny wasn't doing anything illegal. He wouldn't do that."

I smiled to myself. She was about seven years younger than Danny. In high school, she couldn't have known what was going on. And now, maybe she really didn't know or maybe she just didn't want to know.

"Would you be willing to talk to me anyway?" I said. "You never can tell. Something you remember just might help even if you don't think you know anything. I know you think it was just a random shooting, but what I really want to talk to you about is Danny. I just want to know about his life and what he'd been doing in the last eighteen years. That's how long it had been since we'd seen him, except for one time about three months ago when we saw him in a restaurant."

I could hear Bonnie sigh. "Okay," she said. "I'll talk to you, but it'll have to be today and it can't take long. This is my only day off and I have a lot to do."

"That's wonderful," I said, trying to hide how excited I was. "What time would be good for you?"

Bonnie hesitated for a few moments. "Well, I was going to go into Philadelphia this morning, but I ought to be back by lunchtime. Do you want to meet me at my place for lunch, say around 1:30?"

"Sure," I said. "Can I bring anything?"

"No, I have everything I need," she said. "As long as you don't expect anything fancy, we'll be just fine."

I laughed. "Don't worry about it. I'll see you at 1:30."

After I got directions to her place and hung up, I tried Jimmy's home number again. This time I got an answer.

"Yeah?" he said.

"Is this Jimmy Patrinkis?" I said. He sounded so cranky I was almost hoping he'd say no.

"Yeah. Who's this?"

"It's Annie Johnson," I said. "I hope I didn't get you at a bad time."

He hesitated a bit. "No, I just woke up is all. What's up?"

"Well, Dave and I were hoping we could get together with you sometime soon to talk about Danny."

"What about him?" Jim said.

"We think he was murdered."

He laughed. "Where've you been?" he said. "Everyone knows he was murdered. They just don't know who did it."

"No, what I mean is we don't think it was random. We think someone meant to kill Danny. We think they knew who Danny was and they had a reason to want to get rid of him."

There was another pause. "What makes you think that?"

I told him about the letters, but I didn't mention anything about the illegal activity. I was afraid that would scare him off. "It was your mother who showed them to us," I said. "She thinks the same thing we do. In fact, she asked us to try to find the murderer. She doesn't think the police will do it because they're convinced it was random."

Jim let out a long whistle. "Well I'll be a son of a . . . Did she give the letters to you? Do you have them with you?"

"No," I said. "She kept them, but Dave was planning to tell the police about them so they could pick them up." I didn't mention the money. I thought it might be best to keep my mouth shut about that.

He paused again. "Did he call the cops yet?" he asked.

Now I hesitated. I wasn't sure why, but I decided I wanted him to think that the police already had the letters. "Yes," I said, "I'm sure he did."

"All right," he said. "I'll talk to you. What did you have in mind?"

I was just about to tell him about my lunch appointment with Bonnie, but then I changed my mind. "I'm sort of tied up until at least three today, but if you're free anytime after that, it would be great," I said.

"How about four?" he said.

"Four's fine," I said. "Just tell me where."

Jim gave me his address and as soon as we hung up, I called Dave. "We have to give those letters to the police," I said in an urgent voice.

"Calm down," Dave said. "Why do we have to do that? What's the rush?"

"Well, didn't you call them about the money?"

"I didn't get around to it yet. Why are you in such a hurry all of a sudden? Nobody but us knows that it's there."

"No, but Jim Patrinkis knows about the letters now, and he seemed awfully interested in knowing if we had them or not. When I said no and told him you were going to turn them in to the police, he wanted to know if you'd done it yet. I'm afraid he's going to go over there and get them."

"Do you think he has something to hide?" Dave said.

"I don't know, but he sounded kind of wary. I'm going to see him at his place at four today. Do you think you could come?"

Dave thought for a moment. "I could meet you there," he said. "Give me the address."

"Do you think you could call the police?" I said after I gave him directions. "You can tell them about the letters and the money. I'll do it if you don't want to."

"No, I'll do it," Dave said. "But why don't you call Mrs. Patrinkis and warn her? I don't want to scare her. If she doesn't know the police are coming, she won't know what's happening."

"She's going to be awfully upset when she sees that money," I said.

"Don't worry about it," Dave said. "I'll explain to the cops that she doesn't even know it's there and that it would upset her if she did. I'm sure they'll keep quiet about it. I'll just tell them where everything is."

"Okay," I said. "Let me know what happens."

As soon as I hung up, I called Mrs. Patrinkis. A woman whose voice I didn't recognize answered the phone. When I asked to speak to Mrs. Patrinkis, she said that Mrs. Patrinkis was sleeping and that she didn't want to disturb her. She asked if I wanted to leave a message. I tried to explain that it was very important and that I needed to speak to Mrs. Patrinkis personally but the woman (who then identified herself as a housekeeper) wouldn't give in. I told her there was no message. There was no way I was going to entrust that kind of information to a perfect stranger.

Dave called me back ten minutes later. "I called them and they're on their way over. Did you call Mrs. Patrinkis?"

"Yes, but I couldn't talk to her," I said. "She has some sort of housekeeper who said she was asleep and wouldn't wake her up."

"Well, then maybe she won't wake her up when the police come either," Dave said.

"That's true," I said. "We can only hope. How did the police sound when you told them about everything?"

Dave laughed. "Like they always do. They seemed real interested in who I was and you too, I'm sorry to say. But it turns out the guy had heard of us because of the other two cases, so I think that helped a lot. I think he was turning us into suspects before I gave him our names."

"Great," I said. "That's all I need is to be a suspect in another murder case. Once in a lifetime is one too many times for me. Oh, by the way, I'm having lunch with Bonnie at her place at 1:30. I don't know if she'd appreciate my inviting someone else, but do you think you'd like to be there?"

Dave sighed. "Well, I'd like to hear what she has to say, but you can always fill me in later. I think you might be right about her not appreciating an uninvited guest. How did she sound when you asked to see her?"

"Okay," I said. "She seemed a little shocked at first that his murder might not be random, and she doesn't seem to believe that Danny could have been doing anything illegal."

"She probably just didn't know about it," Dave said. "I'll see you at Jim's place at four. You can tell me about Bonnie after we leave. I'll take you to dinner."

"You're the best," I said.

As it turned out, I learned a lot more that day than I'd expected to.

CHAPTER 6

I cleaned my kitchen, powder room, and bathroom and painted two footstools before I had to leave for Bonnie's place. She lived all the way on the other side of town in a neighborhood that had a few trees in every block and kids playing in the street despite the windy, overcast day. Bonnie's house was a two-story, red brick square with no porch or even a stoop. She had a chain-link fence surrounding her tiny front yard and a few patches of grass. The rest was dry dirt with loose weeds and branches blowing about. It reminded me of one of those old western movies with dust and tumbleweed all over the place. I was a little early, about seven minutes, but I knocked anyway. Bonnie answered the door with a dish towel in one hand and a baby on her left hip. The baby was dressed in a pink flannel, one-piece jumpsuit with tiny white roses on the collar and cuffs and couldn't have been more than six months old.

I grinned. "I didn't know you had a baby," I said. "She's so cute." I held out my finger and the baby took it in her tiny fist and held on so tightly I thought I'd never get it back. Bonnie started walking toward her kitchen, and I had no choice but to follow since the baby still had a vicelike grip on my finger. I don't know where the little thing got the strength to do that.

Bonnie smiled. "I have five kids," she said. "Four under the age of six and the oldest is eleven."

"Oh, that's right," I said. "I knew that. Your mother mentioned it. Where are the others?"

"They're down in the basement in the playroom my husband built for them. Tara's watching them. She's my eleven-year-old." Bonnie winked at me. "My built-in babysitter, but she says she's more like an indentured servant."

I laughed. "It keeps her out of trouble, I'll bet."

"You got that right," Bonnie said. "If you wouldn't mind holding Sarah for a minute, I'll get our lunch on the table. It's just chicken salad sandwiches and potato salad. You're not a vegetarian, are you? I guess I should've asked."

"Oh, no," I said. "Chicken salad is great. In fact, it's one of my favorites. My aunt used to make it with pickle relish and Miracle Whip on rye bread."

Bonnie smiled. "Well, I'm afraid I don't have the pickle relish and I used real mayonnaise, but I do have rye bread if you prefer that."

"That would be great," I said.

Bonnie handed me the baby, which made me about as nervous as I could be. I've never had a baby myself, and I don't have any nieces or nephews since I was an only child, so this was a new experience for me. I enjoyed most of it too, all except the part where she spit up on my sweater. I never did get that out and I tried three times.

Bonnie put a plate with a sandwich, red potato salad, and pickles before each of us and asked if I'd like iced tea or a Coke. I went for the Coke. Then she took the baby from my arms and sat at the table, holding her on one knee while she ate.

After I'd taken a few bites, she looked at me shyly and said, "How is it? As good as your aunt's?"

I grinned. "It's perfect," I said. "Really good." I liked Bonnie's personality. She was friendly and reasonably comfortable with me, not at all arrogant or snotty. Of course, I'd only spent ten minutes with her.

"What did you want to ask me about Danny?" she said. "I'm not sure if you remember this, but I am seven years younger than he was, so I wasn't really aware of what was going on in his life most of the time. He graduated high school and moved out of the house when I was only eleven, so I was just a kid the whole time he was at home."

"I know," I said. "I guess what I was hoping is that you might have had a close relationship as adults. You didn't live very far apart. Your whole family still lives in the same town where you grew up."

"That's true," Bonnie said, "but to tell you the truth, I never really saw that much of Danny. Jim and Danny were a lot closer. Of course, they're both guys and they're almost the same age. They're only one year apart."

"How much did you see of him in the last six months or so?"

Bonnie thought for a moment while she shifted the baby to her other knee. "Well, it's a little hard to remember." She gave me a sheepish sort of look. "I was always so busy with the kids and my job and all. You know how it is. You want to get together more often, but you just keep putting it off and then it just never happens. I feel really guilty about that now that he's gone. I keep thinking that if I had known how little time we had left, I'd have spent more time with him."

I gave her a comforting look. "No one ever knows," I said. "People never expect anyone to die, at least not right then. You shouldn't feel guilty. You're no different from anyone else."

Bonnie smiled at me but I could see she was fighting back tears. "Well, thanks," she said. "You're right about one thing. Death sure does take you by surprise, especially when the person isn't even old or sick. But I do the same thing with Ma and she's old. I know she's not going to last much longer, and I still don't get over there often enough. I think she resents it too, which makes me feel even worse. Danny was the only one who really spent any time with her."

I sighed and tried to get onto another subject. "You said it was hard to remember how much you saw of him. Can you give me a reasonable guess?"

Bonnie shrugged. "Maybe two, three times in the last six months."

"Where did you see him?"

Bonnie arched an eyebrow. "Actually it was here each time. He stopped over just on an impulse, I guess."

"How did he act? Did he look like anything was bothering him?"

"I suppose he did act a little funny," she said. "I mean, just the fact that he stopped over that way was a little funny in itself. He'd never done that before."

"You mean he'd never just dropped in on you?"

"Never," Bonnie said.

"So what did he talk about? How did he look?"

"He looked nervous," Bonnie said. "Kind of edgy. But he didn't really talk to me. I'd ask him to stay for dinner, but he always said he didn't have time. I think he really just came to talk to Art. He didn't even seem interested in the kids."

"Art?" I said.

"My husband," Bonnie said. "Every time he stopped by, he spent at least half an hour talking to Art and then he'd leave."

"How did he look when he left?"

Bonnie frowned. "I don't know," she said. "Kind of like he looked when he got here. Sort of agitated, I guess."

"Did Art ever tell you what they talked about?"

Bonnie shook her head. "No, he never told me. He refused to tell me. Said I was better off not knowing. It would only make me unhappy."

"Do you have any idea what he meant by that?"

"I don't have a clue," Bonnie said. "I even asked Danny once when he came by again, but he pretty much said the same thing."

I rubbed my forehead with the palm of my hand. I looked around Bonnie's kitchen. It appeared to have been recently renovated and it was almost spotless.

"Bonnie, when I talked to you on the phone, you said you were sure that Danny was not involved in anything illegal. Why did you say that?"

Bonnie pressed her lips together. "Because I'm sure he wasn't," she said. "Why else would I say it?" Her tone was defensive and her face was a little flushed.

I was afraid I'd upset her even more by my next question, but I really felt I had to ask it. "Did you have the impression that Danny was in some sort of trouble and that he came to Art for help?"

Bonnie had tears in her eyes now and she was jostling the baby up and down on her knee. "What are you suggesting?" she said. "That my husband was doing something illegal? Because if you are . . ."

I interrupted her. "No," I said in a kind voice. "I'm not suggesting that at all. What I was really thinking was that Danny had come to him for help because *he* was in some sort of trouble, not that your husband was."

That seemed to calm her down a bit but not much. "Well, he wasn't. Neither of them were. I don't know what they were talking about, but it wasn't anything illegal, so you can just get that out of your head right now." She wiped away a tear. I was starting to feel sort of guilty.

"Well, let me ask you this," I said. "*If* Danny had come to your husband for help, do you think he would have helped him? Would he be likely to do that?"

Another tear escaped and she brushed it away. "Yes, Art was always very fond of Danny. Jim too, for that matter. He is very protective of people. It's just his way."

"Do you think he'd be willing to talk to me?" I said.

At that, she burst into tears and didn't stop for over a minute. By the time she did, the baby was wailing and I could barely make out what Bonnie was trying to say.

"What did you say?" I asked her as I leaned closer.

"I said my husband's dead. He can't talk to you."

I took a deep breath and held it for quite some time. "I'm so sorry," I finally said. "I'm sorry. I didn't know. No one told me."

Bonnie shook her head and wiped some fresh tears from her cheeks.

"How did he die?" I said.

"He was killed by a hit-and-run driver." Bonnie was sobbing again and the baby was screaming more loudly than ever. I really had to strain to hear her. "It happened in the middle of the day. Broad daylight. But nobody could identify the other driver. They never found him."

I stared at her. "When did this happen?" I said.

"About four weeks ago," she said.

Only three weeks before Danny died.

CHAPTER 7

I arrived at Jim's house at ten minutes to four, and Dave was there waiting for me in his truck. He started to get out when he saw me, but I motioned for him to get back in. Then I went around to the passenger side and hopped in next to him.

"What's wrong?" he said.

"I have something I want to tell you before we see Jim. Bonnie told me that her husband, Art, was killed by a hit-and-run driver only about three weeks before Danny was killed."

Dave's eyes widened. "Did they ever find the driver?" he said.

I shook my head. "Nope, never did. Is that a strange coincidence or what?"

Dave let out a small laugh. "Yeah, I'd say so. What else did she tell you?"

"She said Danny came to their house a few times over the last six months and that it was really unusual for him to do that. In fact, he'd never done it before without calling first. And she said he spent almost the whole time talking to Art, and neither of them would ever tell her what they talked about. They said she was better off not knowing. But she still insists there's no way either of them would have been involved in anything illegal."

Dave gave me a little smile with the left side of his mouth. "People sure can be blind when they want to be, can't they?"

I shrugged with one shoulder. "Well, we'd better go in," I said. "We can talk more about this later. I don't want Jim to see us out here."

It was just starting to rain and the wind was strong enough to make walking a little difficult for me. Dave put his arm around my shoulders and pulled me close. Jim's neighborhood was about two miles from the Ben Franklin Bridge, a pretty rundown area I wouldn't want to be alone in at night. Many of the buildings had been torn down, leaving several vacant lots in every block. Most of those were covered with broken glass and trash. Jim's place was a two-story apartment building with no lock on the front door and no light in the hallway. It was already beginning to get dark, and it was hard to see the numbers on the doors. We had to light matches to see them. Jim was in apartment three, which turned out to be on the second floor. The stairs were so old that they leaned to one side. I was glad there was a railing to hold onto because I wasn't sure I'd have been able to keep my balance otherwise. I could smell a combination of deep-fried food and urine which almost made me sick.

We knocked on the door and heard Jim say, "Come in. It's open." Not a good idea in that neighborhood, but I wasn't going to be the one to point that out.

When we opened the door, I spotted Jim on a sofa covered with a faded cotton throw, smoking a cigarette and drinking a can of beer. He had the TV on and seemed to be pretty involved in what was going on.

He motioned to us without taking his eyes from the screen. "Sit down," he said. "Take a load off. You want a drink?"

We both said no at once.

He took his eyes from the set, looked around for his remote, and switched the TV off. Then he got up and turned on some lights. The apartment was small and dingy with graying wallpaper, a gray-green rug that I guessed had been plain green at one time, and old, mismatched furniture. There was a naked lightbulb hanging from the ceiling, an overfilled ashtray on a coffee table ringed with glass marks, and magazines and other papers strewn everywhere. A normal guy's place from what I could see.

After he'd turned on every lamp in the room, he sat down on a chair near where Dave and I were seated. He looked relaxed and pleasant, not the least bit annoyed at our being there. I was relieved to see that.

"So, what can I help you with?" he said as he looked from me to Dave. "I sure would like to know who killed Danny, but I don't know how I can help you. I'll be happy to try, though."

I smiled at him. "That's all we ask," I said.

He smiled back but it looked a little strained. "So what can I do for you?" he said.

Dave took over from there. "Donna says that Danny was involved in something illegal, but when we asked her to tell us more about it, she said she really didn't know anything. But she told us to ask you. She says you know all about it."

Jim's face turned red and he tightened his jaw. "Donna doesn't know what the hell she's talking about," he said.

Dave gave Jim a hard look. "Why would Donna make up a story like that?" he asked. "She seemed sure that you knew all about it. We're just trying to find Danny's killer, and information like this may help us do it. If you know something, I think you should tell us."

Jim glared at Dave but he didn't say a word.

"You're afraid of someone, aren't you?" Dave said.

Jim took his eyes from Dave's face and stared across the room. He still didn't say anything.

"Jim, we know all about the car thefts when Danny was a kid. I have a feeling you knew about them too. Was he doing the same thing again?"

Jim put down his beer with a thud and looked at Dave. "You're getting into something that can't do you any good," he said. "You're not going to find Danny's killer, and you may end up just like him."

"Is that a threat?" Dave asked.

"No, man, that's a warning!" Jim said with a combination of anger and frustration.

"You're involved too, aren't you?" Dave said.

Jim clenched his jaw again.

"How else would you know so much?" Dave said.

Jim took in a deep breath and slowly blew it out. "Let me put it this way," he said in a low tone. "Whether or not I'm involved in anything is none of your business, and it's got nothing to do with Danny's death. I want you to understand one thing. These are people you do not want to mess with. Do you hear what I'm saying?

Nobody's going to tell you nothing and you might get hurt. Just stay out of it. You got nothing to gain by risking your life."

"But if you suspect someone," I said, "why don't you just tell the police?"

"And what if it doesn't check out?" Jim said. "What if they find out I was the one who set the cops on them, but the cops can't nail them? Then where will I be?"

I didn't have a good answer for that.

"What does Art have to do with all of this?" Dave asked.

Jim's eyes opened wide and he sat up a bit straighter. "What do you mean?" he said. "What about Art?"

"Annie went to see Bonnie," Dave said. "Bonnie told her that Danny came to see Art a few times in the last six months and that something was obviously bothering him. But when Bonnie asked Art about it, he wouldn't tell her anything. He said she was better off not knowing. And she says Danny told her the same thing."

I could see that Jim's breathing had quickened, and he was staring off into space with a bewildered look on his face.

"Was Art involved in the same thing that Danny was?" I asked. When Jimmy shot me a look, I said, "You don't have to tell me what it was. Just tell me if you know if Art was involved."

Jim shook his head. "No, he sure wasn't," he said. "He didn't have anything to do with it." Jim had that sort of look people get when they're running a confusing idea through their head for the first time.

"Jim," Dave said, "do you have any idea what Danny could have been talking to Art about?"

Jim breathed in and out a few times. Then he just sat

there in silence for what seemed like minutes. "I might," he finally said.

Dave and I nearly pounced on him. "Well, what was it?" I said.

"Danny worked for the American Delivery Company," he said. "Several months before he was killed, he was accused of stealing some of the packages that he was supposed to be delivering. People were complaining that they weren't getting their merchandise, and so the company started looking into it. Since Danny's was one of the routes, he got suspended until they figured out what was happening."

"Did they ever find out?"

"No," Jim said. "Well, not on their own, anyway. But Danny didn't want to sit around doing nothing, so he started doing a little investigating on his own. He was pretty sure Chuck Dombrowski was the one stealing the packages. He and his cousin Roger Thornton both worked for the company too."

I wrinkled my brow. "They went to our high school, didn't they?"

"Yeah," Jim said. "They were both in my class."

"So what happened?" Dave said.

"Roger was sure it was Chuck, too, and turned him in. Chuck got fired and Danny went back to work."

"You don't think Chuck could have killed him for that, do you?" I asked.

Jim gave me a look. "I hardly think so," he said. "What's the big deal? It wasn't even Danny who turned him in. Roger was the one who did it. If he was going to kill anyone, it would have been Roger."

I couldn't argue with that reasoning.

"But what does that have to do with Art?" Dave said.

"I'm not sure," Jim said, "except that Art worked for the same company. Maybe Danny asked Art for money. He was asking everyone else."

"Did he ever ask you for money?" I asked.

Jim hesitated a moment. "Yeah," he said. "He came to me with that letter. He was crazy with fear."

"Did you give him any?" I said.

"I gave him five thousand. I did the best I could. It was all I could spare."

I smiled. "That was a lot of money. I'm sure you did what you could."

Jim didn't smile back, but his expression softened a bit.

"Did he tell you what he thought the letters were about?" I asked.

"He didn't know," Jim said.

"But he must have had some idea who they were from," I said.

"He wasn't sure of that either."

"Then how did he think he was going to get the money to these people?" Dave said. "If he didn't know who they were, how would he know what to do with it?"

"He figured they'd contact him again and tell him what to do."

"Did they ever do that?" I said.

"Not as far as I know," Jim said. "Day after I gave him the money he was dead."

I looked at Dave and frowned. "Do you know if they found the money on his body?" I said.

Jim sighed with a look of disgust. "It wasn't part of his personal effects," he said, "and I sure wasn't going to bring it to their attention, if you know what I mean."

I nodded. We talked awhile longer, but Jim refused to give us any more information on whatever he and Danny were involved in, and I can't say I blamed him. If he was right, he might end up in the same position as Danny, and we still might not know who did it. I didn't want to feel responsible for someone's death, so I didn't push the matter any further.

When Dave and I reached the car, he asked me where I wanted to go to dinner.

"How about Don Pablo's?" I said. "But how can you think of food at a time like this?"

Dave gave me one of his crooked smiles. "For someone who knew exactly where she wanted to eat, that's some question."

I felt myself blush, so I changed the subject. "What do you say we go and talk to Chuck and Roger?" I said.

"Just what I had in mind," he said. "Should we call ahead or just surprise them?"

I laughed. "Well, I'd love to surprise them, but we don't even know where they live."

"Don't worry about a thing," Dave said with a grin. "I know exactly how to find them."

CHAPTER 8

The next morning, I watched while Dave called the American Delivery Company and impersonated Roger Thornton's elderly father, claiming that there was a personal family emergency and that he needed to find Roger immediately. Believe it or not, it worked. The guy gave Dave a description of Roger's route, including the approximate times he might be found in particular locations along the way.

"But we don't even know what he looks like now," I said after Dave hung up.

"We don't have to," he said. "We'll know it's him because he'll be in the truck."

Roger was due at Seventh and Pine in Philadelphia at 2:00 P.M. This was in Center City with a lot of row homes that had been fixed up and went for a pretty high price. Pennsylvania Hospital and a few others were nearby, so we could park in one of the lots and then hang out on the corner until he showed up. We could grab him when he got out of the truck.

We both decided to get some work done until we had to leave, so we agreed that Dave would be back at my place at 1:00 P.M. and we'd drive there in his truck.

I cut out a shelf I had just designed, glued it together, sanded it, and gave it a base coat of paint. While that was drying, I cut out another shelf and did the same thing with that one. By that time, the first one was dry, so I gave it a second coat and then started on a third shelf. I went back and forth among them until I had fully painted and stenciled all three.

Each one was different. The first was a creamy ivory with little pink roses along the outer sides. The second was pale green with lilacs in place of the roses, and the third was light yellow with a string of white and yellow daisies. They were all so beautiful I couldn't decide which one I liked best. Not only that, I wanted to keep them all for myself. That's one of the drawbacks of my business. I have a hard time giving up what I make.

I had fifteen minutes to spare when I was done, so I made myself a hard-boiled egg sandwich with Miracle Whip on whole wheat toast and a cup of tea.

"Ready to go?" Dave said when I opened the door ten minutes later.

"Just about," I said. "Just let me grab my coat."

Apparently the noon hour is a bad time to find a parking space in the lot I had in mind. The lot was entirely full, but we didn't know that until we'd driven through the whole thing. We had to go several blocks away to find a space and then run all the way back to Seventh and Pine in order to make it on time.

"What if we already missed him?" I said when we

reached the corner, gasping for breath.

"So we'll try again tomorrow," Dave said.

We had waited fifteen minutes and I was just about to give up when the familiar pale green American Delivery Company truck pulled around the corner and stopped two doors down. A trim, middle-aged man with dark hair and a little gray at his temples got out and went around to the back of the truck.

"Do you think that's him?" I whispered to Dave.

"Hey, Rog," Dave yelled, and the man turned to look at us.

"Looks like he's our man," I said.

Roger looked at us with a confused smile. "You talking to me?" he said.

We walked toward him and Dave held out his hand. "Dave Barrio," he said. "This is Annie Johnson. We were in Danny Patrinkis's class at Camden High."

A look of recognition spread over Roger's face. "Oh, yes," he said. "Sure." Then he frowned. "But what are you doing here?"

"We were hoping for a chance to talk to you," I said. "About Danny."

Roger opened his mouth and closed it again. Then he let out a little laugh. "I hope you weren't counting on doing it now," he said in a slightly amused voice. "I'm running late already, and there's no way I can stop before I finish my route. I'd lose my job."

"No, no," I said. "We only wanted to find you so we could set up something for a later time."

"How's tomorrow night sound to you?" Roger said. "I'd say tonight, but my wife's sister and her family are coming for dinner."

"Tomorrow's fine," I said. "You choose the time and place."

Roger chose his house at 7:30 P.M.

*   *   *

The next night Dave picked me up at seven and we headed for Roger's place. He lived in Collingswood, a homey little town in Camden County with sidewalks and trees and an atmosphere from the Fifties. His house was a two-story colonial with medium-blue siding and white trim. He had a big oak tree in the front yard and another on the side of the house.

We rang the bell and a woman answered. She was about our age with short blond hair worn in a pageboy style, a body and clothing that reminded me of Marilyn Monroe, and deep-set bright blue eyes. Her smile showed a set of straight white teeth.

"Hi, I'm Marsha," she said. "You must be Annie and Dave. Come on in. Roger's waiting for you."

Three children sat on the front room floor watching a television that was turned up to a blaring pitch. I don't know how any of them could stand it. Roger was in the room with them, calmly reading a magazine. When he saw us, he stood up and came toward us.

"Why don't we go downstairs?" he said. "It'll be a lot quieter."

Roger took us down to the basement, which was carpeted and paneled and nearly soundproof. There were three fish mounted on the wall, a computer, a large desk and filing cabinet, a worn couch and three easy chairs, a coffee table, and another TV suspended above a bar. Behind the bar was a sign for Hamm's beer with a bear, a fish, and a running stream.

"Where did you get that sign?" I asked Roger with a big grin.

He smiled too. "My grandfather gave it to me. He had it above his bar when I was a kid. It has to be at least forty years old, possibly fifty."

I nodded, the grin still on my face. "My grandfather had one just like it," I said. "I haven't seen one since I was ten."

Roger moved behind the bar and opened a refrigerator from down below. "Would you like something to drink?" he said. "I don't have anything alcoholic but I have a lot of different sodas." He rummaged around and I heard the clink of bottles. "I have orange, lime, cream soda, root beer, and Coke," he said.

Dave laughed. "I'll take a root beer," he said.

"And I'll take lime."

Roger put two bottles of I.B.C. root beer and one of Stewart's lime on the bar, opened them, and handed each of us a glass from a shelf behind him. Then he waved his free hand toward the couch and chairs. "Let's sit over there," he said. "It'll be a lot more comfortable."

We moved to the other side of the room and sat down. I sneaked a look at Roger as he took a swig of root beer from the bottle. He seemed perfectly relaxed and at ease with us. I was glad to see that. When someone's nervous, I'm more inclined not to trust them to tell me the truth.

Roger looked from Dave to me. "So you're trying to find Danny's killer," he said in a matter-of-fact tone. "I have to give you credit. That's gotta be a hard thing to prove. A runaway driver that no one ever identified. How do you think you're going to be able to find him?"

I took a deep breath and let it out. "Well, when you look at it that way," I said, "it does sound like an almost impossible job. But we're not planning to approach it from that angle. We're just going to talk to everyone we can and see if we can find out what was going on with him during the time before his death. I figure if we can do that, we might find out who had a motive to kill him."

Roger raised his eyebrows. "Guessing at a motive is a long way from proving someone's guilty, though, don't you think?"

"Absolutely," said Dave. "But it's a good place to start. We'll worry about the rest as it comes."

Roger nodded a few times and took another swig of soda. "Well, it sounds like you know what you're doing. I have to hand it to you. I wouldn't have known where to start." Then he wrinkled his brow. "I want to help, of course, but I'm not sure what you want from me."

"We know about the trouble Danny got into at work," I said, "and that you were the one who discovered that it was Chuck Dombrowski who was stealing the packages instead of Danny."

Roger blinked and sat up a little straighter. "Well, let's put it this way," he said. "I discovered that Chuck was one of the guys lifting the packages. That doesn't mean that Danny wasn't doing it too."

I frowned. "But then why did they let Danny go back to work after Chuck was caught?"

"Because Chuck was taking packages from Danny's route, so it looked to the company like Danny had to be innocent and Chuck was the guilty one."

"Then what makes you think Danny could have been doing it too?" Dave said.

Roger shrugged. "I guess now that I think about it, it would have been pretty hard for him to run his own route and take things from another route at the same time. He really couldn't have done it on the days he was working."

"Do you know if any of the packages on his route were

taken on the days he was working?" I said.

"Yeah, I know they were," Roger said. "That's one of the reasons they suspected Danny in the first place. That and just the fact that it was his route, of course."

"You said there were others suspected," Dave said. "Who were they?"

"I'm not sure who they were," he said. "I only know about Danny because he was a personal friend."

"You mean he told you about it?" Dave asked.

Roger nodded. "He came over to the house the night it happened. He couldn't understand why they wouldn't give him a chance to prove he was innocent before they fired him. They didn't really have any evidence on him. It was really nothing more than a guess."

"But a sort of logical one," Dave said.

Roger shrugged. "Well, sure, but I understood how Danny felt so I told him not to worry. We'd figure out who was really doing it."

"How did you do it?" I said.

Roger laughed but it was a sad one. "On my day off the next week, I drove Danny's route the whole day. For the first hour or so I just followed the driver they'd assigned to take over for Danny. But then I stayed behind him and parked every so often. About three hours later I saw Chuck steal one of the packages that hadn't been taken in by the resident." Roger shook his head. "I just couldn't believe it at first. I guess I didn't want to believe it. I don't know if you know this, but Chuck is my cousin."

I nodded. "Yeah, we did know that. It must have been kind of hard for you to turn him in."

Roger gave me a look. "You know, it might have been if it wasn't for the way he acted when I told him about what happened to Danny. He wasn't the least bit sympathetic, and he acted like he was so sure Danny was guilty. When I told him he wasn't being fair because there wasn't any real evidence against Danny, he started bringing up old stuff from the past. Like that had anything to do with it. Sure, Danny got himself into trouble when he was a kid, but that had nothing to do with this. They were separate things. You have to give a guy credit for reforming."

"So you know about what he was doing back in high school," Dave said. His tone of voice made it a statement rather than a question.

Roger stared at Dave and didn't answer right away. His look was guarded and I wondered why he'd be reluctant to talk about that now unless maybe he was involved in the same thing.

"Yeah, I knew," he finally said. His eyes were still on Dave's face, watching him carefully.

"How did you know about it?" I said.

Roger shrugged. "What difference does it make?" he said. "We're talking about way back in high school. I don't see how something that happened that many years ago could have any bearing on Danny's death."

That was the first time it occurred to me that it might.

"Do you happen to know who else was involved?" Dave asked. "Back in high school, I mean."

There was a slight hesitation. "I might," he said. "But like I said, I don't see why it matters."

"Well, what if your suggestion is right?" I said. "What if it is possible that something that happened way back then could have led to his being murdered now?"

Roger rolled his eyes, but then he paused as if he suddenly took my idea seriously. "I guess it's possible," he said, still sounding like he didn't believe it. "But it seems pretty far-fetched to me."

"Well, how about humoring us for the moment?" I said. "Assuming it is possible, can you tell us who else was involved?"

Roger sucked in his cheeks and looked across the room. I gave Dave a questioning look but he just kept a straight face.

"His brother Jim was, but I'm sure you knew that," Roger said.

"We did," I said. "Was there anyone else?"

Roger paused again. "Chuck was in on it too," he said. His voice was so soft I could barely hear him.

CHAPTER 9

I stared at Dave and then at Roger. "You mean Chuck was stealing cars back in high school with Danny and Jim?" I said.

Roger nodded. "There were some other people involved too, but I don't know who they were. They were older. I think they were the ones that were responsible for selling off the parts and getting rid of the remains."

I kept quiet for a bit and thought about what Roger had said. "Do you have any idea if Chuck is still doing that sort of thing?" I said.

Roger looked surprised by my question. "No," he said, "I doubt that he is. Why do you ask?"

I looked at Dave.

"Because Danny was still doing it," Dave said.

Roger gave Dave a sharp look. "How do you know that?" he said.

"From Jim," I said. "He wouldn't come right out and admit anything, but it seemed pretty obvious from the way he was acting that he knew all about it and that he was just as involved as Danny was."

Roger stood up and started to walk in circles. "I wonder if it's the same guys they were working with in high school," he said.

I didn't say anything and neither did Dave.

"Did Jim say anything about Chuck being in on it?" Roger asked.

"Not a word," I said. "He never mentioned him at all. On the other hand, he never really admitted that he was doing it or that Danny was, for that matter. We never asked him about Chuck."

Roger nodded and kept moving.

"Jim told us that these guys were dangerous," Dave said. "He told us we shouldn't mess with them or we might get hurt."

Roger stared at Dave. "Are you saying he was threatening you?" he asked with a confused expression.

"I don't think he was threatening us," I said. "I took it more as a warning. The impression I got was that he knew these people and he had reason to believe that we should be afraid of them. I think he might be afraid of them too."

Roger blew out his breath but didn't say anything.

"Did Chuck ever say anything to you about the other guys in this business being dangerous?" I said.

"No," Roger said. "But now I'm talking about high school. From what you just said, it sounds like Jim was talking about now, and that could be a whole different group of people."

"Well, that's true," I said. "Do you have any reason to believe that Chuck is involved in it now?"

"It hadn't occurred to me until you brought it up," he said. "Chuck certainly never mentioned it to me, if that's what you're asking."

"Does he seem to you like he's been in some sort of desperate need for money?" Dave said.

Roger let out a little laugh. "Well, I don't know if it's need," he said. "It could be nothing more than greed. Chuck was always the kind of guy who wanted more than he had and when he got it, he still wanted more. He was never satisfied. Just the fact that he was taking the packages shows he was looking for ways to pad his income."

"What happened after you turned him in?" I said.

"The company decided not to report it to the police, but it was in exchange for his resignation. They also insisted he pay for what was taken, but he's still fighting them on that part."

"What did he do with the things he took?" I asked.

"I think he sold most of them," Roger said. "And I assume that he couldn't pay for them because he'd already spent the money."

"Do you have any idea how much was taken? In terms of value, I mean."

"The company claims it was close to a hundred thousand dollars' worth of merchandise," Roger said.

Dave whistled. "They have insurance, don't they?"

"Sure," Roger said, "but they got hit with a big increase in premiums and it took awhile before the insurance company would even accept the claim. Most of the residents were insisting on being reimbursed before the insurance money came through. So the company was trying to get Chuck to pay up, but he didn't have it anymore. He probably hadn't been able to get rid of anything at its retail price anyway. They were selling stolen goods and he had to get rid of them fast. He'd have to take anything he could get for them."

"Do you know where he was selling them?" I said.

Roger laughed. "He got rid of a lot of it by setting up one of those carts in Center City Philadelphia. People can sell anything down there and nobody seems to care. He got away with it, at any rate."

"How did you find out about all of this?" Dave said.

"Well, like I told you, I discovered it was him just by following Danny's route. Then I confronted him with it, and he tried to get me to go in with him on the deal. He was telling me all about it. You know, like how much money he was making and all that. He said, 'Hey, you're family. I'll let you in on the deal but you gotta keep quiet.' I was so disgusted I just started to walk out on him. Then he started yelling at me and telling me how I never did amount to anything because I wasn't willing to take any risks and that Danny was the same kind of worthless wimp that I was. That's when I lost it and decided to turn him in."

"Did you tell him you were turning him in?" I said.

"No," Roger said, "but I'm sure he figured it out. He knew I was going to Danny about it so when he got called on the carpet, I'm sure the first person that came to mind was me." Then he frowned. "By the way," he added, "just in case he doesn't know it, I'd appreciate it if you wouldn't say anything."

"No problem," Dave said. "Did you ever find out who any of the other guys were who were doing the same thing?"

"No, I never did," Roger said. "I'm not sure it matters, though. What difference could that make?"

"None probably," I said. "Did you ask Chuck about them?"

"I never thought to ask," Roger said. "I doubt he would have told me anyway. And I didn't really care who the others were. The only reason I was interested was because of Danny. Danny was a good friend from way back, and I didn't want to stand by and watch him fry when I knew who was really responsible."

"I'm sure Danny appreciated that," I said.

Roger gave me a sad look and attempted to smile. "Yeah, he did. He was very grateful. I just wish I could do something for him now, but I still don't see how a drive-by shooting could have any connection to all this."

"It would if the person doing the shooting knew Danny and was doing it because of something we've been talking about."

"Yes, but like what, for instance?" Roger said.

"We haven't figured that out yet," I said, and Roger let out a little laugh. "But we'll let you know when we do."

We left Roger's place at about 8:20 and both of us were hungry. "How about a pizza?" Dave said.

"Sounds good," I said, and Dave headed for our usual spot. The weather had cooled off quite a bit and there was a slight drizzle. Dave turned on the windshield wipers and put on the heat.

Our favorite pizza place is only five blocks from my house. It's privately owned by a couple in their forties. The woman inherited it from her father three years ago and she made a few changes which I think helped the business a lot. When her father ran the place, it was sort of dirty and rundown and the pizza wasn't very good.

And that was all they served. Now the pizza's much better and they have garlic bread and a whole bunch of appetizers. And everything is clean and cheery with red-checked curtains and tablecloths and those drip candles in empty wine bottles. It may not be very original but it makes you feel really comfortable when you're there and you want to stay awhile. They're always playing Italian music in the background. It's all so relaxing.

"So what do you think?" I said after we'd sat down at our regular booth. "What should we do next?"

"I was thinking we should try to see what we can get out of Chuck," Dave said. "He seems to be the guy with the most information about everything we've heard so far."

"But why would he be willing to share it with us?" I said.

Dave shrugged. "Who knows?" he said. "It's always worth a try. Have you ever noticed how almost all the people we question in these investigations end up talking to us at least on some level? Some talk more than others, but we always seem to be able to get them to talk."

I laughed. "I guess you're right, now that I think about it. Maybe we should take a little trip to American Delivery Company and see if we can get anything out of them. I'd love to find out who the other package stealers were, or at least who was suspected."

"I doubt if the company would share that kind of information with us," Dave said. "I'm sure they consider it confidential."

"That may be true," I said. "But we might be able to get some of the other drivers to talk. There must be someone over there who knows something. I'll bet there was a lot of talk among the other drivers while all this was going on. They were probably all pretty interested in who did it."

Dave looked at me and nodded. "You're right," he said. "They had to have been interested. It's human nature. And I'll bet they'd be all too happy to chat about it now that it's over."

"Assuming it *is* over," I said. "We don't know that for sure. There could be someone out there who hasn't been caught and who could feel he has an awful lot to lose by talking to us."

Dave wrinkled his forehead. "Let's go over there first thing tomorrow morning," he said. "If we get there early enough, maybe we can catch some of the guys before they leave on their routes."

CHAPTER
10

At six the next morning, Dave pulled up in front of my house and I ran out to meet him. "I brought us some coffee and doughnuts," he said when I got in the car.

I grinned. He had those big powdered-sugar-covered doughnuts and a thermos of hot coffee with just enough non-dairy creamer. Just the way I like it. "You are the best," I said as I reached for a doughnut and three napkins.

We had to drive quite a distance to the lot where the drivers pick up their trucks and check in for the day. It was in south Philadelphia but luckily in an area that Dave seemed to know pretty well. When we got there, we could see at least a dozen delivery men dressed in the pale green uniforms. Some were already in their trucks and others were hanging out in the parking lot and talking. It was perfect. Just what we needed. Dave pulled up next to a group of men and rolled down his window.

"I wonder if any of you can help me," he said. "Did any of you know Danny Patrinkis?"

The guys looked at each other before they answered. "Sure," one of them finally said. "I knew him. Actually, we probably all know who he is now. He was killed a few weeks back."

Dave told them who we were and explained how we came to be involved in the murder investigation. "We're interested in finding out anything we can about this package-stealing business," Dave said. "Do any of you know anything about that?"

Most of the guys started looking at their feet. "Only what we've heard," said the one who had answered us earlier. "Supposedly there were at least three routes where guys were stealing packages, but only one guy was actually caught in the act. The other two were just assumed to be guilty because the packages were taken from their routes."

"Do you mind if I park my truck and talk to you a little more?" Dave said. The rain had stopped, and it was almost pleasant outside except that it was much colder than I'd expected and I hadn't dressed for it.

"Sure," said the guy who'd been talking to us. He looked willing but not thrilled at the idea. I noticed that a few of the others in the group left and got in their trucks as soon as Dave pulled away.

When we got back to what was left of the group, Dave directed his questions at all three of the men. "The way I understand it," he said, "is that Danny Patrinkis was also assumed to be guilty until someone caught Chuck Dombrowski in the act. Then they let Danny off the hook and fired Chuck. Isn't that right?"

One of the men who had not yet spoken held out his hand to Dave. "I'm John Fleming," he said.

"Dave Barrio," Dave said back. Then he introduced me.

"You heard it the way we did," John said. "Someone turned Dombrowski in. He'd actually tailed him through Patrinkis's route and caught him in the act."

"Then why does the company still assume the other two guys are guilty just because the packages were taken from their routes?" I said. "It seems to me that they'd have figured out that if someone else was taking the packages from Danny's route, the same thing could be happening in the other two cases too."

"That's what the other two guys argued," said another guy. He introduced himself as Ralph. "But no one would listen to them."

"Sounds pretty unfair to me," I said.

"That's what we all think," Ralph said. "And I know one of the two—guy named Fred Maxwell. He's as honest as the day is long. There is no question in my mind that he didn't do it, and it's tearing him up having people think he could have. Hasn't helped his home life any, either."

"You mean his wife thinks he's guilty?" I said.

"No, I don't think that's it," Ralph said. "It just put a strain on the relationship. He's out of work now and they have six kids all under the age of seven. She's at her wit's end. Of course, I can't say I blame her, but it's not Fred's fault by any stretch of the imagination."

"Do you think he'd be willing to talk to us about this?" Dave asked.

Ralph took a deep breath and a little smile crossed his face. "You can give it a try," he said, "but he's not too sociable these days. I'm lucky if I can get two words out of him. I was just there last week and he wouldn't even look at me."

"Would you mind giving us his address and phone number?" I said. "I promise we won't bother him if he doesn't agree to it."

Ralph thought for a moment. "Yeah, sure," he said. "So long as you keep your promise." I pulled a scrap of paper and a pen from my purse, and he scribbled the information on what little room was available.

Then he held out his hand. "I really have to be going," he said. "I wish you luck, and please give Fred my best." Then he stopped. "Let me take that back. Please don't tell him where you got his number if you wouldn't mind. I wouldn't want him getting angry with me."

I smiled. "Don't worry," I said. "We won't say a thing."

The other two men started to say good-bye when I interrupted. "Do either of you know the name of the third man?" I said.

"Dan Albright," John said. "But I don't know him and I have no idea how you can reach him."

I looked at the other man and he just shrugged.

"Do either of you know anything that might help us?" I said.

"No," said John.

"Sorry," said the other guy, his answer overlapping with John's.

"Well, I have to be going too," John said. "I hope I've been of some help."

"Thanks, you have," Dave said.

John and the other man walked toward their trucks. John got in his, turned around to wave to us, and drove off. After John was out of sight, the other man came back. "Hold on a minute," he said in a low voice. He introduced himself as Clint Farrow. Dave and I patiently waited for him to continue.

"I think I might be able to help you," he said. "I know Dan Albright and I can tell you how to find him. I also know he is guilty. What's more, so is Fred Maxwell. He may have been honest back when things were going well, but when the going got tough, old Fred was willing to do just about anything to feed his kids and please that spoiled brat of a wife he's got. She'd bleed him dry if she could. Sort of what she did, depending on how you look at it."

I found another piece of paper and asked Clint to write Dan Albright's number on it. He couldn't remember the phone number but he knew the address so he gave me that. "The number's in the book," he said.

"How do you know these guys were guilty?" I asked Clint.

Clint looked around in what I'm sure he thought was a casual way to make sure no one was listening. "Albright told me," he said. "He actually thought I might be interested in getting in on it. This was before anyone got wind of it, of course."

"How long were they doing it before anyone caught on?" I said.

Clint let out a sarcastic laugh. "They were going full force for at least eight months before anyone noticed a thing. Of course, they started small, figuring folks wouldn't catch on as quick if they did it that way, and I guess they were right. But then the companies that sell the merchandise started making a stink because the customers complained to them, of course, not to American. Well, pretty soon people were putting two and two together and figured out it was someone with American who was doing the stealing. That's when the company started investigating and determined whose routes most of the stuff was coming from."

I frowned. "You said most of it. What did you mean by that?"

"Well, there was some overlap into other routes," Clint said. "Like with Albright's route, for instance. There was some overlap into the routes surrounding his. And the same was true for the other two."

I nodded.

"Interesting," Dave said. "Did Albright tell you Maxwell was involved?"

"He didn't have to," Clint said. "Maxwell was there at the time Albright brought it up. He was so furious with Albright for telling me, I thought he was going to kill him."

"Do you mean that literally?" I said.

"Well, no," Clint said. "I mean I just thought he was angry enough to do it."

I frowned at him and he gave me an exasperated look back.

"It's just a figure of speech," he said. "An expression. I didn't mean he was really thinking of killing him. Don't go off half-cocked now thinking Maxwell killed Patrinkis. He may have needed money but I can't see him as a killer. No way."

"Okay," I said. "I just wanted to be sure I understood you."

"Did either of them say anything about who the third person was?" Dave said.

"No," Clint said. "Albright probably would have told me but Maxwell's reaction was so extreme that he just clammed up after that. Besides, I told them I wasn't interested anyway. I like the finer things in life just as much as the next guy, but I prefer to get mine the legal way. It's safer that way."

I smiled. "A lot safer in some cases."

"Did Albright ever say anything to you at a later time about either Danny Patrinkis or Chuck Dombrowski?" Dave asked.

"No," Clint said, "and I never brought it up. I figured it was off-limits after the episode with Maxwell."

"Do you know if the company ever asked Albright or Maxwell if they knew who the third person was?"

"I have no idea," Clint said. "Or let me put that another way: it'd be my guess that they did ask that question. It may be how they found out it was Dombrowski rather than Patrinkis."

"And you're sure there were only three?" Dave said.

Clint hesitated as he looked at Dave. "I guess I don't really know for sure," he said. "We all just assumed it was only the three of them. Let's put it this way. They were the only ones that were caught and the only ones suspected as far as any of us knows. Maybe that's a question you ought to ask the company, but I don't know that you'll get anything out of them."

"Well, we're sure going to try," Dave said. "Thanks for your time, Clint."

CHAPTER
11

The American Delivery
Company complex took up at least half of a city block.
There was enough space to hold dozens upon dozens of
the smaller delivery trucks and who knows how many of
the larger ones. Most of the garage area was closed, so we
couldn't see how many of the trucks were still on the
premises. The main office was made of cinder blocks and
had large glass double doors framed in steel. Men were
walking in and out and almost all of them looked in a
hurry. I'd never seen so much pale green in one place in
all my life.

When Dave and I walked into the office, the three men
coming out gave us curious looks. Inside it was bright and
warm, a nice contrast to the dreary wet weather outside.
Three women sat at desks about five yards apart and a
man in a short-sleeved yellow shirt and blue tie was
walking our way. Dave held up his hand to get his
attention. The man smiled and he and Dave shook hands.

"What can I do for you?" he said. He had a white plastic pocket protector in his shirt pocket that contained two ballpoint pens.

Dave introduced both of us and told him we had been close friends of Danny Patrinkis. As soon as Dave mentioned Danny's name, the man stiffened and swallowed hard.

"I'm Mark Goldwin," he said in a serious voice. "Why don't we talk in my office?"

He led us back through a hallway littered with boxes stacked at least a foot over my head. We reached a room at the end of the corridor and he opened the door. More boxes were stacked inside but otherwise the room was pretty tidy. Gray metal file cabinets lined the walls and the top of the maple desk was free of clutter. There was a wooden chair in front of the desk and another behind it. He offered one to each of us but Dave said he'd stand, so I took the one in front of the desk and Mr. Goldwin took the other.

"Now," he said. "What is this all about?" He looked so stern I felt like I was back in school in the principal's office.

I gulped and Dave took over. "We're trying to find out who killed Danny, Mr. Goldwin."

Goldwin's eyes narrowed and he glared at Dave. Before he had a chance to say anything, I cut in. "We don't suspect anyone here," I said. "That's not what we're here for. We do need to know what was going on during the last few weeks of his life, though, and we were hoping you could help us. We know he was accused of stealing packages from some of the people on his route, but he was later found innocent. Can you tell us anything about that?"

"That's company business," Goldwin said. "I can't discuss the matter with you."

"Can you tell us why you didn't go to the police?" Dave said.

Goldwin sucked in his cheeks. "I told you, that is company business. I'm afraid I can't help you." He stood and walked around to the front of the desk. "I'm a busy man," he said. "I'll have to ask you to leave now."

"Have you had incidents like this before?" Dave asked as he ignored Goldwin's request.

Goldwin swallowed hard and didn't answer.

"Well, I'm sure you won't mind if we mention it to the police," Dave said. "I think they'll find it may be relevant to their investigation." Dave nodded to me and we started to leave. Before we were out the door, Goldwin called us back.

"Hold on," he said. "Let's not get carried away here."

Dave and I turned around but remained standing in the doorway.

"Please," Goldwin said. "Come back and sit down."

We hesitated a bit but then walked back in. I took the seat I'd had before and this time Dave took the one behind the desk. That seemed to throw Goldwin off guard a little. After closing the door, he moved about the room and finally decided to lean against one of the file cabinets.

"I made a deal with my men—the ones who were involved in this thing—not to report it to the authorities if they could guarantee a return of everything they took or the fair value of whatever they can't return. If I go back on my word, we may never get anything back."

"Have any of them returned anything?" I asked.

"Yes," he said, "and I'm confident we'll be getting more. The threat of the law is quite an incentive, as you might guess."

"Wouldn't the law require them to pay it back anyway?" I said.

Goldwin wrinkled his brow. "I have no idea," he said, "but I can't afford the risk of finding out."

I gave him a little smile. "What about Chuck Dombrowski?" I said.

Goldwin gave me a blank look. "What about him?"

"How much has he paid back?"

Goldwin let out a heavy sigh. "Very little," he said. "He claims he sold everything for far less than it was worth and then spent all the proceeds."

"Then why would you deal with him at all?" Dave asked. "Why not turn him in to the police?"

"Because of the others," Goldwin said. "There were three in all. If I turn Dombrowski over to the police, he may turn in the other two. If that were to happen, I'm afraid I wouldn't get anything more from them. They've returned some of the original merchandise, and they've agreed to pay us what they can on a monthly basis until they make up for the entire loss."

"How are they able to do that without jobs?" I asked.

"That's not my concern," Goldwin said. "My concern is for the company. It's their own doing that they're out of work. They brought that on themselves."

"Well, I can't argue with that," I said, and Goldwin's expression softened.

"Can you tell us anything about Danny as an employee?" Dave said. "Had he ever gotten in any trouble outside of the package-theft episode?"

Goldwin sighed. "Ordinarily, I wouldn't answer that," he said, "even though Patrinkis is dead. But since the answer is no, I don't feel that I'm betraying anything confidential. The truth is that he had been a model employee the entire time he'd been here. We were quite surprised when we discovered—or, should I say, *believed*—that he was in on the thefts."

"What about the others? Were you surprised about them too?"

Goldwin frowned. "Yes, as a matter of fact we were. They had all been model employees. Not a one of them had a mark on their records previous to that."

"Do you think Chuck Dombrowski intentionally made it look like Danny was the guilty one?" I asked.

Goldwin opened his right palm. "I have no doubt," he said. "Why else would he steal from Patrinkis's route instead of his own? He had to know that the first one we'd suspect was Danny since the packages were taken from his route."

"Then what about the other two?" Dave said. "Why would they be so stupid as to steal from their own routes when Dombrowski wasn't?"

Goldwin stared at Dave for several moments. "I don't know the answer to that," he said.

"Do you think it's possible that Dombrowski set the other two up?" I asked.

Goldwin wrinkled his brow. "Well, no. Of course not," he said. "They've admitted to doing it. Like I told you, they even returned some of the merchandise. They couldn't have been set up."

"Unless someone threatened them or paid them to confess to something they didn't do," I said.

Dave turned and looked at me, and Goldwin frowned. Then he shook his head. "That's not my concern," he said. "My only duty is to get back what was lost."

I sighed and looked at Dave. He read my face and stood up. "We're going to get going now, Mr. Goldwin. You were very helpful. Thank you for your time."

Goldwin walked us out and wished us luck but didn't offer to be of further assistance if we should need him.

"What do you want to do now?" Dave asked when we got back in the truck.

I looked at my watch. It was barely after eight and we'd already had coffee and powdered-sugar doughnuts. "Want to go out for breakfast?" I said.

Dave laughed. "Sure. Where to?"

"How about Jerry's Diner?"

"Sounds good to me," he said.

Jerry's Diner is on the corner of Fifth and Beecham just outside of Camden and it's my favorite place for breakfast, my favorite meal of the day. Jerry's serves it around the clock so we often go there late at night when we get the urge. The outside is red and green with chrome trim. It's pretty gaudy but that's part of what I like about it. The inside has green and yellow lights, and it makes your food look awful but you get used to it.

We sat in a booth near the window and the waitress brought us a large pot of coffee and a pitcher of orange juice right away. I ordered a western omelet with cheese, toast, and potatoes and Dave ordered the same. You may be thinking by now that I must be overweight. Well, I'm not. I'm just a little past skinny and not even halfway to plump. Besides, I don't always eat like this.

"Who would you like to talk to next?" Dave said.

My eyes lit up. "I was thinking Fred Maxwell," I said. "That guy named Ralph was so convinced he was as innocent and honest as they come."

"And Clint Farrow said just the opposite," Dave added.

"Right," I said. "And he wasn't too fond of Fred's wife, either." I got another glint in my eye. "Maybe we should try to talk to her first. It might be interesting to see what she'd have to say—especially if Maxwell doesn't know we're going to talk to her."

Dave smiled. "And how do you propose to manage that?" he said.

I smiled back. "I have my ways," I said.

CHAPTER
12

Ralph had told us that Fred Maxwell had six children and that he was still out of work. Clint Farrow had told us that Fred's wife wasn't the most pleasant person to be around. I knew I was taking my chances, but it was my guess that Fred Maxwell would probably experience an irresistible urge to get out of the house at some time during each and every day.

After Dave dropped me off, I filled a thermos with coffee (I hear private eyes always do that on a stakeout) and drove to Fred Maxwell's house. He lived in Williamstown, a small town about fifteen to twenty minutes east of Camden if you take the expressway and the traffic's not too bad. The house was a white frame with green trim and red shutters. Christmas decorations from the year before filled the yard, roof, and windows. There were a Santa and his sleigh on the roof but only two reindeer. The yard was covered with little Santas, enormous candy canes, wise men, an oversized nativity scene, an artificial tree, and three golden angels. An old pale blue Buick was parked in the stone driveway. The sky was still overcast and there were lights on in the front of the house. I parked across the street about half a block away, took out my magazine, scrunched down in my seat, and waited.

An hour had gone by and no one had come out of the house. I'd had to look up from the magazine every few words so I wasn't even getting anything read. Two hours after that, I had to go to the bathroom. I figured I could either give up and find some place to go or act like a real detective and stay put. Of course, you know what most real detectives are able to do, but I didn't have the right equipment, if you know what I mean. I was just about to go clear out of my mind when a man wearing a muted plaid corduroy jacket and faded tan corduroy pants came out of the house. He had the jacket zipped to his neck and the collar pulled up. His shoulders were raised and his head was down. He walked right by me and didn't even notice. I waited until he was three blocks away and got out of the car. I took another look just to make sure he wasn't watching and walked down the pathway to the front door. I could hear children's voices inside and not one of them sounded the least bit happy. I took a deep breath and rang the bell. After what seemed like minutes, a woman answered. She gave me an annoyed look as soon as she opened the door.

"Whatever it is, I'm not buying any," she said.

I smiled. "I'm not selling anything," I said. "Are you Mrs. Fred Maxwell?"

She frowned and stood very still. "Yes?" she said quietly.

"I didn't mean to worry you," I said. "I just want to talk

to you for a few minutes." I told her who I was and how I was involved in investigating Danny's death.

She hesitated a moment and then asked me to come in. I guessed that she was in her early thirties, but she appeared older when I first looked at her. I think it was because she seemed so tired and overworked. Her hair was a dark blond. She wore it short, about chin length, and it was pushed behind her ears. She had no makeup on and her jeans were old and baggy. Her red plaid flannel shirt must have once belonged to her husband.

The house was small and smelled of popcorn. There were toys everywhere. Papers, coloring books, and crayons littered the floor, and crackers and cookies were left on tables and even chairs. The furniture was all relatively new, however, and obviously bought as a set. I counted five children in one room and each was talking louder than the last. I really felt sorry for her. I don't know how anyone can take care of that many kids, a house, and a husband, especially with no income. Clint Farrow was entitled to his own opinions, but I had a feeling there were good reasons for any behavior he saw as unattractive.

I gave her a warm smile. "I'm sorry for bothering you, Mrs. Maxwell. I really need to talk to your husband. Is he home?"

She shook her head. "Please, call me Rita. Fred went for a walk. He says he can only take so much of this." She let out a little laugh as she waved a hand to take in the room and the children. "I don't think it ever occurs to him that I might need to get out too."

I smiled and nodded. "I just wanted to ask him about Chuck Dombrowski and Dan Albright," I said.

At the mention of their names, Rita started.

"You know them, don't you?" I said.

I could see her jaw tighten. "Yes, I know them," she said.

"I take it there's no love lost between you," I said with a sarcastic smile.

She rolled her eyes. "You can say that again. If those men ever set foot in this house again, I swear I'll kill them."

"So they've been here before?"

"Oh, yes," Rita said. "Many times. They're good friends—or at least they were."

"You mean they're not friends anymore?"

Rita shrugged. "I'm not really sure," she said. "All I know is Fred hasn't talked to anyone since it happened."

"What did he tell you about it?"

Rita took in a deep breath and let it out. When she got tears in her eyes, I started to say something but she stopped me. "It's all right," she said. "Just give me a moment. This isn't easy for me to talk about." She took a tissue from a box on the top of her refrigerator and blew her nose. "I'm sorry," she said. "I don't know why I let it get to me so much. I think it's partly because I always thought Fred was such an honest person. It was one of the things that attracted me to him in the first place. He was always so open about his feelings and if you asked him something, he'd tell you the truth. Or at least it seemed that way. Ever since this happened, I've started wondering if he's ever telling the truth."

I gave her a sympathetic smile. "Has he talked with you about it?" I said. "I know you may think he wasn't telling you the truth when he did, but I'd still be interested in hearing what he said."

She shrugged again. "Mostly he just said he was talked into it. And the worst part was he said he did it for us." She got tears in her eyes again. "I just couldn't believe he said that. It was almost like he was blaming me and the kids. Like if it weren't for us, he wouldn't have done something like that."

"Did you need the money? Is that what he meant?"

Rita nodded. "We've always needed money," she said. "And that was another thing. Why now all of a sudden? We weren't any worse off than we'd ever been. We never had any money for extras—you know, like going out or things like that—but how much of that can you do with six kids anyway? And Fred never complained. He wasn't the complaining type."

I couldn't help remembering what Clint had said about her. I certainly couldn't see any evidence of it myself but I needed to say something. "You don't think he thought you wanted more, do you?" I asked as if I were certain it wasn't true.

Rita frowned. "If he did, I don't know where he got the idea. In fact, he was always saying he wished he could give me more, and I'd tell him I had all I needed right here with him and the kids. I don't know how he could have gotten it in his head that I wanted more than we had. I told him time and time again that I didn't."

I shook my head. I was really confused at that point about Farrow's comment so I decided to just ask her about him. "What do you know about Clint Farrow?" I said in as innocent a voice as I could.

"He's one of Fred's closest friends," she said.

"Have you met him?"

"Sure. He used to come to the house all the time. Why do you ask?"

I shrugged. I didn't really know what to say. "What do you think of him?" I said. I wasn't sure what I was fishing for but it worked.

Rita laughed. "Well, he never liked me much, I can tell

you that. He and Fred may have been close, but I could barely stand him and the feeling was mutual. According to Fred, Clint doesn't really like women, and he especially doesn't like women who stay home with their kids. He was married for twenty years, and now that he's divorced, he has to pay a lot of alimony because his wife never worked. They had four kids and she stayed home with them. I don't know what he expected her to do, but I think I remind him of her, so he's always sort of short with me."

I laughed. That wasn't the answer I'd expected, but it was better than some of the ones I'd guessed at.

"How long was your husband involved in this package stealing thing?" I asked.

"I'm not really sure," she said. "He'd been acting kind of strange for at least six months, though, and we seemed to have more money during that time so that's probably when it started."

"Can you remember when that was?"

"Well, it was just about six months before they all got caught," Rita said. "So that was about seven-and-a-half, eight months ago now."

"Did you ever see any of the merchandise?"

Rita looked startled, as if the thought hadn't occurred to her until then. "No, come to think of it, I never did," she said.

"Did he ever tell you what he did with it?"

Rita shook her head. "That's something you'll have to ask him," she said. "I didn't ask and I don't want to know."

"But he owes the company a lot of money, doesn't he?"

"Yes," she said in a sad voice. "I don't want to know that either. I never asked him how much, and I never asked where he's getting it from."

Just then, Fred Maxwell walked in the door.

CHAPTER 13

Fred Maxwell came in through a mud room that was attached to the kitchen and took off his boots and jacket. He started to say something to Rita but stopped when he saw me.

"This is Annie Johnson," Rita said. "She was a friend of Danny Patrinkis. She wants to ask you a few questions about him. She and a friend of hers are trying to find out who killed him."

Fred looked at me with a blank expression, walked over to the kitchen counter, removed a towel from one of the drawers, and wiped the rain from his face. He placed the towel on the kitchen table and left the room without saying a word. I looked at Rita and she gave me an apologetic look.

"Let me talk to him," she said quietly.

She left the room and I took a seat at the kitchen

table. I could hear their voices, but I couldn't make out what they were saying. A few minutes later, Rita came back and sat down with me.

"He hasn't talked to anyone since it happened," she said. "He refuses to talk to you too. I'm sorry. I tried but he just won't budge."

"Would you mind if I tried?" I said.

She winced a bit but then changed her expression. "Well, I suppose it can't hurt," she said. "But don't expect much. He hasn't even talked to Clint, and they're best friends. Every time he calls, Fred tells me to tell him he's sleeping or out for a walk."

"Do you think anything happened between the two of them?" I said.

Rita thought for a moment. "I don't know," she said. "I think he probably just wants to be left alone because he's ashamed of what he was doing. I keep trying to tell him that he needs friends now more than ever, that they'll help him through this, but he's not like that. When something's bothering him, he just shuts everyone out, even the people that care about him the most. I told him if he keeps it up, someday people will just stop trying. He doesn't listen, though. He never does. He shuts me out with the rest of them."

I gave her a sympathetic smile and patted her arm. "Well, I'll give it a shot," I said. "He may open up if he feels it might help us find out who killed Danny. Were they very good friends, do you know?"

Rita frowned. "I'm not sure," she said. "He was very upset by his death, though. He must have known him well enough to care. Of course, when I asked, he wouldn't talk about that either."

I smiled briefly and left the room. Fred was sitting

amongst five of his children, watching television. Bugs Bunny was on and he was staring at the screen as if the next world war were being reported. He was on the couch and the kids were all on the floor, so I was able to sit at the opposite end of the couch. He didn't even move when I sat down. I waited almost a minute to see if he'd say anything but he didn't. He hadn't even looked my way.

"Mr. Maxwell," I said. "I know this is hard for you to talk about, and I would never ask you to do it if it weren't for a very important reason."

He continued to stare straight at the screen. The children had begun to notice me, though, and two of the littlest ones climbed up on the couch in between Fred and me. I smiled at them and said hello. They both gave me very shy smiles back and even shyer hellos.

"I need to find out whatever I can about Danny," I said to Maxwell. "I need to know what was going on with him before he died. We know he was very afraid of someone and that he was desperate to raise money, and we think that has to be connected to his death somehow. One of the things he got mixed up in is this package-stealing thing, and that's where I'm hoping you can help me."

As I spoke, Fred shifted his position but his gaze remained fixed on the screen. He took several deep breaths and slowly let them out.

"Were you friends with Danny?" I said. "Did you talk to him about anything at all in the weeks or months before he was killed?"

Fred sighed and lowered his head. Then he started to speak, but his voice was so quiet that I had to ask him to raise it because I couldn't hear him.

"He asked me if I could tell him why Chuck

Dombrowski chose his route to steal from," Fred said.

"What did you tell him?" I said.

"I told him the truth," Fred said. "I didn't know. I hadn't even known Chuck was in on it."

"But you knew about Dan Albright, didn't you?"

Fred nodded.

"Then why wouldn't you know about Chuck?"

"How can I answer that?" he said. "I don't even know how many there were altogether. All I know is three of us were caught and Dan Albright was behind the whole thing. He was the one who came up with the idea."

"Then how did you get in on it?"

"He approached me one day and asked if I wanted an easy way to make a little extra money. I said 'Sure,' not knowing what he was talking about. When he told me, I said I wasn't interested. But then he started talking about my kids and how I was letting my wife down by making her work so hard to take care of them and never being able to give her anything. And he told me we weren't really taking anything that wouldn't be replaced because the company's insurance would cover it. I still said no but he kept working on me. A few days later I called him and told him I'd do it."

I thought about what he'd said for a few moments. "Why would Dan Albright care so much if you did it?" I said.

Fred let out a short and bitter laugh. "Because I had to give him all of the merchandise I took, and he paid me only half of the proceeds after he sold it. The more people he got involved, the better he made out."

"Do you have any idea how many people were involved?"

"No," Fred said. "The only one I knew about until we got caught was Albright. I didn't find out about Dombrowski until later."

"What about Danny?" I said.

Fred looked at me and frowned. "What about him?" he said.

"Do you think it's possible that he really was involved but that it only looked like he was innocent when they caught Dombrowski?"

Fred blew out his breath. "I don't know. I really don't. I suppose that's possible. But if it is, where was Danny stealing from? We already know Dombrowski was taking the packages from Danny's route."

"Yeah, I know. It doesn't make much sense to me either. There's just something about the story that doesn't add up."

Fred shrugged as if he didn't care.

"I know this is a really personal question, but have you been able to pay back any of what you took?"

He laughed his bitter laugh again. "I had a little money saved and I gave the company everything in the account. I also had a load of merchandise that I hadn't given to Dan Albright yet. I don't know where I'll get the rest. I haven't been able to find work. If it weren't for my parents helping out, I wouldn't even know where our next meal was coming from."

"What about Albright?" I said. "Shouldn't he have to pay for some of what you took since you were only getting half of the proceeds?"

"Sure he should," Fred said, "but he's not."

"Why not?" I said. "Doesn't the company know he was behind the whole thing?"

"No," Fred said, "they don't, and I'm not about to tell them."

I gave him a questioning look. "But why would you let him get away with that? You can't even afford to pay back what you took. Why should you pay for part of what he took too?"

"Because he told me it wouldn't be good for my health."

I gaped at him. "You mean he threatened to hurt you?" I said. "Do you think he was serious?"

"I've got a wife and six kids," Fred said. "I can't afford to find out."

"Well, I can understand that," I said. I looked at his children. There were so many of them and they were all so little. Two of them were arguing about whether Daffy Duck was a boy or a girl.

"Do you think he could've killed Danny?" I said.

"I doubt it," Fred said. "I don't know what motive he could've had."

"Did Albright ever mention Danny to you?"

"No," Fred said.

"When Danny came to see you, did he talk to you about anything other than Chuck stealing from his route?"

"Not on that occasion."

"What about other times? How often did you see him?"

"I ran into him every once in a while. We didn't always talk, but we exchanged a few words every now and then."

"Did he ever say anything about being afraid of someone?"

"No, I'm sure I'd remember that."

"Did he appear to you to be worried about anything?"

Fred thought for a few moments. "He did seem nervous the last time I talked to him."

"When was that?" I said.

"It was a few weeks after everything came to light," Fred said.

"You mean about the packages?"

Fred nodded.

"What did you talk about?"

"Nothing in particular," Fred said, "but he seemed a little jumpy."

I frowned. "What do you mean by jumpy?"

"He kept looking around like he was expecting someone."

"Where were you?"

"In Stanley's Grill," he said, "right across the street from the office. Danny was there from time to time."

"Did anyone come in and talk to him while you were there?"

"No, at least not that I noticed. I was only with him a short time. I'd gone up to the bar to get a drink and he was sitting there. I was just making conversation and he kept looking over my shoulder."

"Did you see him leave with anyone?"

"No," Fred said. "I left myself a short time later. I don't even know if he was still there when I left."

"What about the other times you saw him there? Did he seem jumpy? Did he say anything to you?"

Fred sighed and thought for a while. Then he shook his head. "Sorry," he said. "I really can't remember. Whatever he might have said didn't stand out in my mind. It couldn't have been too important."

"Did he ever ask you to lend him money?"

"No," Fred answered with a laugh. "Everybody knows I have six kids. He'd be crazy to think I could lend him money."

I nodded. Then I suddenly remembered something else I'd wanted to ask him. "Tell me about Clint Farrow," I said. "I understand Dan Albright asked him if he wanted to get in on it."

"Yeah," Fred said in a disgusted voice.

"And he asked him in front of you," I added. "Why do you think he did that?"

Fred looked at me and wrinkled his brow. "I don't know," he said. "It got me really angry, though, because then Clint knew what I was doing. I was ashamed enough as it was. I couldn't bear having him know."

"Is that why you haven't talked to him since you were caught?"

Fred nodded. "I haven't talked to him since the day Dan Albright let him know about it."

"Clint turned it down, didn't he?"

Fred nodded and looked at his hands.

"Do you know if Clint needed money?" I said.

"Yeah, he sure does," Fred said. "He has to pay his ex-wife a fortune in alimony, and he's got child support payments for four kids. He feels like there's almost nothing left of his paycheck after that."

"Which would be why Albright asked him, wouldn't it?"

Fred nodded. "I imagine so. My guess is he went after people he knew were really in need of extra money. Clint certainly fits that description."

"But how would Albright know that about all of you?"

"He was good friends with all of us. He knew what our situations were, just like we knew his."

"What can you tell me about his?" I said.

Fred sighed. "I'd rather not tell you anything if I don't have to. I'd rather you asked him yourself."

"Do you have some reason to be afraid of Dan Albright?"

Fred closed his eyes and shook his head.

CHAPTER 14

The next day was Friday, November 4, and it was cold, rainy, and just plain miserable outside. I made hot chocolate and biscuits for breakfast and spent the day stripping the finish off some secondhand pieces I'd bought at a rummage sale. I do that sometimes. I'll redo something to the point where the original object can no longer be recognized and then I'll sell it. This time I had two end tables, a coffee table, and a set of TV trays. They were pretty boring when I bought them, but by the time I was through with them, they'd be painted and stenciled in the country style I like so much. Dave laughs at some of the things I do (like the cuckoo clock with lilies-of-the-valley all down the sides) but he's usually very supportive.

I worked until four, took a shower, and dressed. Dave was picking me up at five. We were going to Stanley's Grill across from the American Delivery Company offices to see what we could find out.

From the outside, Stanley's looked like a pretty swinging place. The sign was at least five feet high and spread across the entire front of the building announcing Stanley's Grill in bright, neon-green lights. It was completely dark by the time we arrived and the green reflected off the wet pavement. The effect was eerie and sort of fun at the same time.

The inside was dark as bars usually are, and a jukebox was blaring music sung by Celine Dion, a pleasant surprise. There were peanut shells and popcorn all over the floor, bright brewery signs behind the bar, and at least a half dozen blond bartenders (all female and all with really puffy, high hairdos). It was a very large place, almost warehouse size. Near the bar and in the center of the floor were high brown wooden tables with four barstool-type chairs around each. Along the walls were booths that held as many as six people.

"So what's the plan?" I whispered to Dave as we were walking through the door. "Are we going to let people know who we are right away or just try to blend in the background and see if we hear anything?"

Dave spoke into my ear. "Let's do both," he said. "We can have something to eat and pretend to mind our own business and then start asking questions."

It sounded like a good plan, but it didn't turn out as we'd intended it to.

"Well, look who's here," were the first words we heard when we walked in the door. It was Clint Farrow with a few of his buddies.

I smiled and Dave nodded. "Clint," Dave said. I said, "Hi."

We hadn't counted on being spotted so quickly, so we just kept on walking and took a table near the bar. "See anyone else we know?" I said under my breath.

"No," Dave said, "but I'm not going to look now. Let's

just order and try to act cool. I don't want to scare anyone off."

A waitress came over almost ten minutes later and we ordered hamburgers, onion rings, and two Cokes. The place was filled with men in pale green as well as quite a few others who apparently didn't work for the company. There were a few women too, but the men far outnumbered them. After we'd been eating and talking for a while, I started to casually look around. Clint was still there and so were Ralph and John Fleming, the other guys we'd talked with in the lot the other day. I looked for Roger but didn't see him, and I wouldn't have recognized Chuck Dombrowski. Dan Albright I hadn't met yet.

After we were done with our meal, I suggested to Dave that we order another soda and just nurse it until Clint and the others who knew us left. "That way we can talk to people without being watched by them or without their interfering in any way."

"Why would you think they'd interfere?" he asked.

"I don't know," I said. "I guess I'd just feel more comfortable if they were gone."

My plan started to look like a big mistake when forty-five minutes and two sodas later, Clint and his friends still hadn't left. But in another half hour, Clint did leave and the others took off a few minutes later. The problem was that by that time, most of the other guys had cleared out too.

"Well, what do you say?" Dave said. "Should we give it a shot?"

I shrugged and Dave got up and walked toward a group of five men seated at a booth.

When we reached them, one of the guys looked at Dave with a puzzled but friendly expression. Dave held out his hand and introduced us. Then he told them what we were doing and that we needed to find out as much about Danny and about the package thefts as we could. They all looked at each other and shifted in their seats.

"I didn't even know him," one said.

"Neither did I," said another. The other three agreed.

"What about the thefts?" I said. "Do you know anything about that?"

No one answered for a moment and then they all said no at the same time. Looking back on it, it was actually kind of funny.

"Do any of you know Dan Albright?" I said.

There was another hesitation but then the man who'd spoken first nodded his head in the direction of the bar. "That's him over there," he said. "The guy on the far end of the bar."

I looked over at the bar and spotted a very large man with what looked like jet black hair, wearing jeans and an orange T-shirt, sitting alone. "Thanks," I said, and Dave nodded to the group.

"What are we going to ask him?" I said.

"Heck if I know," Dave said. "I guess we'll just have to wing it. Isn't that what we do most of the time?"

I laughed but it was a nervous laugh. For some reason Dan Albright made me more than a little uneasy.

"Dave Barrio," Dave said as he held out his hand to Albright. Albright gave him a funny look and didn't extend his hand.

"We understand you knew Danny Patrinkis," I said. I wasn't sure if that was true but my guess was right.

"Yeah, I knew him," Albright said in a gruff voice. "What about it?"

"We're trying to find out who killed him," I said. "We're talking to anyone we can to see if they can tell us anything about what he was doing during the last few weeks or months of his life."

Albright's expression was a little wary but not hostile in any way. He shook his head. "What do you want from me?" he said, this time in a much friendlier voice.

I took a deep breath. "Please don't get upset about this. We're not planning to reveal this to anyone who doesn't already know about it, but we know that you were the one who organized the package thefts."

Albright stiffened and the blood rushed to his face.

"All I want to know," I said quietly, "is if Danny was involved in the thefts in any way. Was he one of the ones who were taking packages?"

Albright's face and neck were still red, but I could see his shoulders relax a little. "No, he wasn't involved," he said.

I smiled. "So he really was innocent?" I said. "He didn't take any of the packages from his route?"

Albright laughed. "If he did, I didn't know about it. Let me put it this way, he wasn't involved in what we were doing. What he might have been doing on his own I can't tell you."

I sighed. I thought I'd finally gotten one thing settled, and he unsettled it for me just as quickly.

"Can you tell us why Chuck Dombrowski was stealing from Danny's route?" Dave said.

Albright gave both of us a disgusted look. "Dombrowski wasn't working for me either," he said. "Whatever he was doing, he was also doing on his own."

I tried my best not to show my surprise.

"How many people did you have working for you?" Dave said.

Albright stood up at that point, took a dollar bill from

his wallet, and slapped it on the bar. "This is where the conversation ends," he said. "You said you were here to talk about Patrinkis. This has nothing to do with him."

"Why would you keep quiet about the others after you've already been caught?" I said.

"Because I have my principles," he said. Then he turned and walked out.

"Can you believe that guy?" I said to Dave. "Principles. Give me a break."

"What I'm starting to wonder," Dave said, "is how many other routes have had thefts and how much of this the company has kept quiet from the employees."

"Well, if that's true," I said, "I can't understand why they haven't gone to the police. You'd think they'd want it cleared up as quickly as possible."

Dave got a funny look on his face. "Unless one of the management is involved in it too," he said.

I let my shoulders drop. "This is getting too complicated," I said. "And as far as we know, Danny's death isn't even connected to the company. We've been forgetting all about the chop shop."

Dave arched his eyebrows. "You're right," he said. "Not to mention all the usual possibilities."

Like what?" I said.

"Well, Donna's the obvious one. They were still married but not living together. She claims she still loved him, but we saw him with another woman just a few months before he was killed."

"But she's so hostile when she talks about him. It didn't sound to me like she really wanted to get back together with him. I just assumed she was lying when she said that to cover up how angry she was with him."

"That's partly my point." Dave said. "I think she was

angry. But it may have been because she still loved him and knew he was cheating on her. Or maybe everything she said was true. Maybe he really did leave her just to live with his mother and she hated him for that."

"I wonder if Bonnie or Jim know anything about it. We never thought to ask them," I said.

"Bonnie might be the best one to talk to," Dave said. "Didn't you tell me she doesn't like Donna very much?"

I nodded. "She said she was always shooting her mouth off about something. That was when I asked her about Danny being involved in something illegal."

"And then there's the money," Dave said. When I frowned, he explained, "The sack of money we found in his room. We have no way of knowing if that had any connection to either the company or the car thefts."

"But what else could it be?" I said. "We don't have any evidence at all that he was mixed up in anything else."

"The point I'm making is that the money might *be* the evidence. First of all, we know he was in desperate need of money, or so it seemed. And he acted like he needed it fast. If he needed it so fast, why was he still hanging onto that cash? Why hadn't he given it to whoever was threatening him or demanding the money?"

I had to admit I'd never thought of that. "Maybe he was waiting until he had the right amount," I said.

Dave frowned and shook his head. "If he was that scared, he would've given them what he had just in hopes of keeping them satisfied until he was able to raise more."

"Maybe he just never had the chance," I said. "Maybe he meant to give it to them and was killed before he got around to it. Or," I added, "maybe he never found out who was sending him the threatening letters, and he didn't know who to give the money to."

CHAPTER
15

I called Roger Thornton the very next morning and asked him how I could reach Chuck Dombrowski.

He hesitated before he answered. "I doubt if he'll be of any help," he said. "You won't be able to trust a thing he says."

"That's probably true," I said, "but we'd like to try anyway. You never know. We might be able to learn something useful."

"Okay, suit yourself," Roger said. "He's working as a night janitor, so you can reach him at home, days." He gave me his number.

"Thanks, Roger. I'll keep in touch."

"How's the investigation going?" he said as I was about to hang up.

"Terrible," I said. "The more people we talk to, the more confusing it gets."

He laughed. "I'm sorry," he said. "I didn't mean to laugh. It's just that I know what you mean. My wife always says I think too hard and the harder I think the more confused I get."

It was only a little after 9:00 A.M. and since Chuck worked nights, I decided to wait a few hours before I called him. I wanted him to understand what I was saying and I didn't want him to be angry. Then I had an idea. I called Roger back.

"Is Chuck married?" I asked him.

"Yes, why?" he said.

"Is his wife home during the day?"

"As far as I know," Roger said. "She doesn't work."

I thanked him again and dialed Chuck's number. A woman with a very pleasant voice answered. I could hear the sound of a television in the background and the voice of a toddler saying "Mommy" over and over again.

"Is this Mrs. Dombrowski?" I said.

"Yes," she said, still sounding very pleasant. Then she asked me to hold on. I could hear her patiently ask the child what she wanted and then ask her to please keep quiet while Mommy was on the phone.

"I'm sorry," she said. "My little girl is not quite three and she gets terribly jealous when I'm on the phone."

"That's all right," I said with a laugh. "I'm sorry to bother you, but I need to talk to your husband and I know he works nights. I wondered what would be a good time to call him."

"Well, he gets up at five but then he gets dressed and eats dinner. I'd say six would be best but you won't have much time with him. He leaves at 6:15."

I groaned.

"May I ask what this is about?" she said.

I explained the whole situation to her. She made little comments here and there and sounded embarrassed when I mentioned her husband's involvement in the company scandal. "He doesn't like to talk about that," she said. "He says he was set up and he doesn't know by whom. But he insists that someday he's going to find out."

"Had he ever been in trouble before?" I asked.

"Not a day in his life," she said. "At least not that I know of. I suppose he could have kept some deep, dark secrets of his past from me, but I don't have any reason to believe that he did."

"Did anyone ever consider that someone outside the company might be doing the stealing?" I said.

"Well, I think that's the first thing they thought of," she said, "but there was never any evidence of it. And then Fred Maxwell and Dan Albright finally owned up to doing it, and they were with the company."

"Did you think Danny was lying about not being involved?" I asked.

She sighed loudly. "I truly don't know," she said. "I certainly did at first, but when Chuck confessed, I assumed I'd been wrong."

"Do you think your husband would be willing to talk to me?"

"I don't know," she said. "He's very bitter about the whole thing. He's had to take a very large cut in pay. He's working as a janitor now over at the school."

"I know," I said, trying to sound sympathetic. "Roger told me."

Now she was perfectly silent. I had forgotten that Chuck must know that Roger was the one who had turned

him in. I wasn't sure what to say, so I said whatever came
to mind and hoped for the best. "Hello?" I said.

"I'm here," she said.

"Is something wrong?"

"No, I guess not. I just didn't realize you were talking
with Roger."

"Don't you and Chuck get along with him?" I asked.

She let out a tiny laugh. "Yes and no," she said.
"They've been close on and off, but they always seem to
be getting into spats over business deals they plan to put
together but that always manage to fall through. For a
while they won't even speak to each other and then
suddenly they're friends again."

"When was the last time this happened?"

She thought for a while. "It has to be over six years now."

"Have they made up since then?"

"Oh, yes," she said. "They never stay mad for more
than a few months. They're like little boys."

"Do you know what kind of business they were
planning to start six years ago?"

Mrs. Dombrowski hesitated a moment. "I think it had
something to do with old furniture," she said. "They were
going to buy up secondhand furniture, I think, and then
refinish it and sell it."

"So what happened?"

"Nothing. That was the problem. Roger suddenly
decided he didn't want to do it, and Chuck was furious
because he'd already bought a whole truckload and paid
for it himself. Then he was stuck with it, and he didn't
want to tackle the business all by himself. He needed
Roger because neither of them could afford to do it alone."

"So it was a totally legitimate business?"

"Oh, yes," Mrs. Dombrowski said. "Why do you ask?"

"No reason," I said. "I'm just fishing for as many facts as I can. Oh, by the way, does your husband have any idea who it was that turned him in?"

"No," she said in an angry voice, "but he swears he's going to find out somehow."

"Has he said how he plans to do it?"

"No," she said. "I'm not sure he's even serious. I don't think he'd know where to start. But if you and your friend ever uncover it, I hope you'll be good enough to share it with us."

"Don't worry, I will," I said and immediately regretted it. Telling Chuck that Roger was the one who turned him in would serve no useful purpose. I also had an idea it might mess up my investigation somehow.

"Do you think it would be all right if Dave and I stopped by tonight?" I said. "We'd only stay a few minutes."

"I don't know," she said. "He might get mad at me for not telling him first."

"Then how about this?" I said. "You could ask him when he wakes up and then call me to let me know. I'll be home all day."

She hesitated for a few moments. "Okay," she said, and I gave her my number.

As soon as I hung up, I called Dave. "Guess who I was just talking to?" I said.

"Uh, Batman?" he said.

"No, I . . ."

"Superman?"

"Dave, will you stop that?"

He laughed and I did too, though I tried not to.

"I called Mrs. Dombrowski to find out when we could talk to Chuck because Roger told me he works nights as a janitor. And I had a really long conversation with her. He gets up at five and she's going to ask him if we can come over and talk to him at six o'clock. We'd only have fifteen minutes with him because he leaves at 6:15, but it might be worth it anyway. Can you come?"

He laughed again.

"Why are you laughing?" I said.

"Because I never knew anyone who could get so many words out in one breath," he said.

"It wasn't one breath," I said in a defensive tone. It really was, but I wasn't about to admit it. "So what about it?" I said. "Do you want to come or not?"

I could almost see him smile. "Yes, of course I do," he said. "How about if I meet you at your place at ten of five, and we'll wait for them to call. If he refuses to see us, I'm sure we can always come up with something else to do."

I smiled too.

At 5:10, Mrs. Dombrowski called and said that she'd talked her husband into seeing us for a few minutes. She reminded me that he had to leave at 6:15 and suggested that we talk on the phone to save time. I considered it for a moment but decided I'd much rather talk with him in person. I wanted to be able to watch his facial expressions and body language. They so often reveal much more than the words themselves which could be nothing but lies. Luckily, they lived nearby, only five minutes away.

"I'd rather talk to him in person if that's all right with you," I said.

She put her hand over the receiver and I heard a muffled question and response. "That's fine," she said.

"But he says he's leaving at 6:15 whether you're finished with him or not."

"Okay," I said. "We'll be there at six on the dot."

At 5:55, Dave and I grabbed our coats, jumped in his truck, took two rights and a left, drove three more blocks, and were there. The Dombrowskis lived in a row home made of red brick with a black front door that hadn't been painted in quite some time. Most of the black had peeled off, showing a dirty blue underneath. The street was bare of trees, and trash bags lined the curbs along with the familiar yellow plastic recycling bins. I rang the doorbell and, after three attempts, decided it must not work. Dave knocked hard and a few minutes later, a slender and pretty woman came to the door.

She smiled at both of us and I smiled back. "Are you Annie?" she said.

She looked at Dave and was about to add something when I said, "Yes, I am and this is my friend Dave Barrio."

Dave said "Hi," and she told us her name was Pam. She was at least five-feet-seven with dark brown hair to her shoulders and soft brown eyes. Perfectly flawless, bright white teeth. Perfectly flawless, olive-toned skin. She was wearing faded jeans, white sneakers, and an oversized green T-shirt.

"Come on in," she whispered quickly. "He's in the kitchen."

We walked through a small living room with a grayish-brown carpet that was worn through in at least four spots. The furniture was mismatched. There was a black plastic recliner, a soiled rust couch covered partially by a blanket in different shades of red and green, a medium blue-and-pink plaid chair, and a brown throw rug under the coffee table. The coffee table and one of the end tables were a maple color. The other tables were either plastic or dark wood with peeling veneer. There were three pictures on the walls, all of flowers and sunshine and grass.

The kitchen was small with a tiny window in front, a tiny four-burner stove with an oven large enough for no more than an eight-inch cake. There was a yellow-checked, plastic tablecloth on the tiny round table, and Chuck was seated with his back to us on one of the four mismatched wooden chairs. Though he must have heard us come in, he didn't turn around. Pam walked with us to the other side of the table so we could face him and introduced us. He was drinking a cup of coffee with his jacket on and he looked very uncomfortable. I assumed the jacket was for effect, a message to us that he wasn't staying long.

Dave held out his hand and after a moment's hesitation, Chuck took it. He introduced us and told him we'd gone to Camden High for a while in Danny's class, the one behind him. Chuck's face lit up a bit.

"What do you want from me?" he said. "Pam told me why you're here, and I don't know who killed him. I can't even make a guess."

"Do you think it could have anything to do with the package thefts?" I said.

Chuck laughed, and it was a deep, bellowing sound. He was a very big man. He looked far too large for the chair he was in, and I had the feeling it might break if he stayed there too long. His shoulders were as broad as a linebacker's and his neck was thick. He had big, meaty hands that wrapped entirely around the mug he was holding.

"I can't see any reason why someone would kill him over that," he said. "As far as I know, he wasn't even involved in it."

"What makes you think he wasn't involved?" Dave said.

Chuck sighed. "Because he claimed he was innocent and I was the one stealing from his route. He had to be innocent."

"Who was it that fired you?" I said.

"Mark Goldwin. He was my boss."

"Can you remember exactly what he said when he fired you?" Dave asked.

Chuck frowned. "When I came in that day to get my orders, he told me to see him in his office. Then he told me there was an eyewitness who'd reported seeing me stealing merchandise from Danny's route. Then he told me to turn in my uniform, and I was fired."

"Do you have any reason to believe that Mark Goldwin or any other member of the management was involved in this?" Dave said.

Chuck's answer truly surprised me.

CHAPTER 16

"Most of the guys think the management's involved," Chuck said. "Why else are they keeping everything so quiet? If things were any other way, they'd have gone to the police."

"Do you have any idea which members of the management it might be?" I said.

Chuck shook his head. "Naw," he said. "Could be any one of them."

"Have you heard any talk from anyone else? Do any of the other guys think they know who's involved?"

"Not as far as I've heard," he said.

"What about Mark Goldwin? Do you think he could be one of them?"

Chuck sucked in his cheeks and thought for a few moments. Then he shook his head. "I don't know," he said. "He could be. Any of them could be."

"But you don't have any specific reason to believe that Mark Goldwin is one of them?"

"No, I don't," Chuck said.

"What about the other *employees*?" Dave said. "Do you know about anyone other than you, Fred Maxwell, and Dan Albright?"

Chuck hesitated for just a moment before he said no.

"Did you ever talk to Danny after you were fired?" I asked.

Chuck's expression changed from tense to slightly guilty. "Yeah," he said. "He came over the next day, wanting to know why I was stealing from his route."

"What did you tell him?" Dave asked.

"I told him he was just a victim of circumstances," Chuck said. "It was nothing personal."

I took a deep breath and let it out to a slow count of five. "Did you ever write him any letters?" I asked in an innocent voice.

Chuck wrinkled his brow. "Letters?" he said. "Why would I write him letters? What kind of letters?"

"It doesn't matter," I said, "as long as the answer is no."

Chuck gave each of us a funny look.

"How well did you know Danny?" Dave said.

"Not well," Chuck said. "I knew his brother Jim better. We were in the same class."

"Did you hang out together in high school?" I said, trying my best to sound as if we were no longer talking about anything relevant to Danny.

Chuck shrugged. "No," he said in an overly casual voice. "I knew him to say 'Hi' but we never hung out after school."

I nodded. "And you haven't seen him lately?"

"No," he said. "Until Danny's funeral I hadn't seen him since we graduated."

"You talked to him at Danny's funeral?" I said.

"Not quite," he said with a laugh. "I went up to offer my condolences and he wouldn't talk to me. Seems he thinks I was responsible for Danny getting in trouble."

"With the company, you mean."

Chuck nodded. "He walked the other way as soon as he saw me coming."

"Well, don't take it personally," I said.

"Oh, yeah, don't take it personally she says. You try walking in these shoes for a day and see if you don't take it personally."

I did my best to give him a sympathetic smile but made no other response. We talked for a few minutes more and then it was time for Chuck to leave.

"I appreciate your talking to us," I said. "If I think of something else, would it be all right if I called?"

"Sure," he said in a resigned voice. "I wish you luck. I don't know how you think you're going to be able to sort this mess out."

Dave and I both laughed. "Neither do we," I said, "but we're going to try."

"Think he's guilty?" I asked Dave as soon as we were back in the truck.

"Of what?" Dave said. "The murder?"

"Of course," I said.

Dave thought for a moment. "Well, he genuinely seemed like he knew nothing about the letters, so unless the letters have nothing to do with the murder, then I think he's probably innocent."

"Do you think it's possible the letters don't have anything to do with the murder?" I said.

"Anything's possible," Dave said.

"But wouldn't it be too much of a coincidence?"

"Not any more than anything else."

"What do you mean?" I said.

"Well, let's assume the murder has something to do with the company scam. Then the car theft business is just a coincidence. And the same would be true the other way around. If someone involved in the chop shop killed him, then the company thing is a coincidence. And the same is true with Donna."

"I get the point," I said. "So what's next on the list?"

"I'd like to talk to Bonnie and Donna again," he said. "I want to ask Donna if she knew about the money, and maybe we can feel her out to see if she suspected Danny was cheating on her."

"What about Bonnie?"

"I want to ask Bonnie about Donna."

Dave and I drove back to my house and I asked him to stay for dinner. It wasn't quite 6:30, though, and neither of us was hungry, so we decided to see if we could reach either Donna or Bonnie.

"Bonnie's probably not home from work yet," I said. "The post office doesn't close until five and she probably has to pick up her kids from somewhere."

"I'm sure you're right," Dave said, "but I'll bet she doesn't work fulltime with all those kids. I hope her husband had life insurance."

"Well, let's give it a shot," I said. I thought for a few moments, rehearsed what I was going to say, dialed the number, and got no answer. "She's not home," I said. "I wonder who watches the kids while she's at work."

Dave shrugged. "Try Donna," he said.

I went through the same process and got her machine. I didn't leave a message. Now I was getting frustrated. I wanted to talk to someone and I didn't care who it was. I dialed Jim's work number but hung up before anyone answered.

"What are you doing now?" Dave asked with a confused look. "Who were you calling?"

"Jim," I said. "But I decided it would work better to just go see him. What do you think of driving by the garage to see if he's working?" The garage where Jim worked was a lot closer to my house than his apartment was.

Dave sort of squinted at me and said, "I suppose, but he probably won't be able to talk even if he's there. He'll be working."

"And if he isn't there, we can try his apartment," I said, completely ignoring his comment.

Dave sighed and shook his head, grabbed his coat, and handed me mine. He walked quickly ahead of me without another word. I had the impression I had done something to annoy him. I decided to just leave it alone and hope it would go away.

We drove in my car, thinking it would be less conspicuous than Dave's truck, and cruised by the garage. There was no sign of Jim or his car. Then we drove to his place. His car was parked out front, I was happy to see, and there was a light on in the front of his apartment. When I started to get out, Dave put his hand on my arm.

"Hold on a minute," he said. "I think we should talk about what we're going to say before we go busting in there, don't you?" Dave hadn't said a word on the way over and neither had I.

"Sure," I said. "What do you want to ask him?"

Dave let out a groan and banged the back of his head against the headrest on his seat. "You were the one who wanted to talk to him," he said through his teeth. "You must have had something in mind."

The truth was, I hadn't, but I couldn't admit that to Dave. "Well," I said, stalling for time, "I thought we might talk to him about some of the things we were wondering about—like Danny and Donna's marriage. Remember how Bonnie said that Danny and Jim were a lot closer than she and Danny were?"

Luckily, that seemed to satisfy him. "Okay," he said. "Let's go. But this time you can do all the talking. I'm not in the mood."

I rolled my eyes (which he didn't see) and got out of the car. When I knocked on his door, Jim yelled, "It's open," just as he had the first time we were there.

I walked in a little shyly and Dave followed. "Jim," I said, "it's Annie Johnson and Dave Barrio. Can we talk to you for a few minutes?"

"Sure," he said. "Take a load off." He was watching television just like the last time and drinking a can of beer. He kept his eyes glued to the screen. Then he switched off the TV and looked at us. "So what's up?" he said with slightly slurred speech. "Did you find the murderer yet?"

"No, not yet," Dave said. "We're just here to clear up a few odds and ends. Nothing important."

"Shoot," Jim said.

I opened my mouth to say something but Dave butted in. And this was the guy who wasn't in the mood for talking. "I'm not asking this because we think she's guilty," he said. "It's more like we want to be able to eliminate her from the list of possibilities."

Jim gave Dave a blank look.

"What can you tell us about Danny and Donna's marriage?" Dave said. "Do you think they were happy together?"

Jim laughed and couldn't seem to stop for nearly a minute. I looked at the space around him and counted seven beer cans in all, not including the one in his hand.

"They weren't even living together," Jim said. "Danny was staying at Ma's house and they were going to get divorced."

Dave put a surprised look on his face. "Why?" he said. "From what Donna told us, I got the impression she really loved him."

Jim snorted and took another drink. "She had a hell of a way of showing it if that's how she felt. Anytime I saw them together, all they ever did was scream and throw things at each other. It was a bloody disgrace."

"What did they fight about?" I sneaked in before Dave had a chance to beat me to it.

"Everything," Jim said. "You name it, they fought about it."

"Do you think he ever cheated on her?"

"Depends on what you mean by cheating," he said.

I rolled my eyes. "I was using the typical *female* definition," I said. "The one where he's with another woman and it's not purely friendship, but he's committed to someone else."

Jim snorted again. "Sure, he fooled around some," he said with a clumsy wave of his hand. "Everybody does. That doesn't make him a criminal, does it?"

I let out a big sigh. "It might give Donna a reason to be

very angry with him," I said. "She was his wife, and I'm sure she expected him to be faithful to her." I hadn't meant to get so upset but I was letting my own feelings and fears interfere with what I was doing.

Dave glared at me and took over. "Do you know if Donna had any reason to suspect that he was cheating on her?"

Jim shrugged. "She was always accusing him of cheating. All women are paranoid about that sort of thing."

"For good reason," I said under my breath, and Dave glared at me again.

"Did you ever hear her accuse him of being with any specific woman?" Dave asked.

Jim sighed and burped at the same time. "Yeah, plenty of times," he said. "It didn't mean anything."

"Was there anyone he was seeing right before he died?" I asked.

Jim waved his hand at me. "Yeah, he had a couple on the side." He had a stupid smile on his face and I was having a hard time looking at him.

"Do you know who they were?"

"I don't remember names," he said with a laugh. "A couple of other details I might recall, but not the names."

"So you have no idea how we could find them?"

"Nope. Can't help you there," he said. "Anything else?"

Dave said no and got up to leave, but I wasn't through yet. I suppose I should have given more thought to my next question but I didn't have time. "Do you think we could talk to some of the guys you steal cars with?" I said.

Dave looked like he was going to kill me and so did Jim. "Are you out of your mind?" Jim said. "You don't want to get involved with those guys. Trust me on this."

"Do you think they could have killed Danny?" I said.

Jim ran his hand across his forehead and I could see sweat on his brow. He swallowed hard. "I don't know and I don't want to know."

"How can you keep working with them when you think they could have killed your brother?" I said.

"How can I not?" he screamed at me. He stood up and started to pace. "What am I supposed to do? If I accuse them and they're guilty, then I'm dead meat. If I accuse them and they're not guilty, I could still be dead meat. My hands are tied."

"Why don't you just go to the police and not say anything to these people?" I said.

"You think they're not going to know who put the cops onto them if they get called in for questioning? He was my brother. How stupid do you think they are?"

"What if we call the police?" I said.

The sweat was pouring down his face at that point, and he was starting to look a little sick. "You can't do that," he said in a shaky voice. "You're not listening to me. You go to the police, the first person they're going to think of is me. They're going to think, 'Who could have told the cops about us? Who would know?' And the first person who comes to mind is Jimmy Patrinkis."

I was starting to see his point. "Okay," I said. "I understand."

Jim kept pacing for another minute or so and finally sat down. We just watched him and kept quiet. After he appeared to have calmed himself down, we said good-bye and left.

"I think we should follow him," I said as soon as we got outside.

Dave stopped, took me by the shoulders, and twisted me around to face him. "I want you to get one thing straight," he said. "*You* are not following him. *We* are not following him. Didn't you hear a word he was saying?"

"How else are we going to find out who these guys are?" I said.

"We're not," he said. "And even if you found out where and who they are, what are you going to do—waltz on in there and say, 'Hi, I'm Annie Johnson and I think you killed Danny Patrinkis'?"

I was beginning to see his point too. "Okay," I said. "Maybe you're right." I hadn't totally given up on the idea, but I knew I had to keep it to myself. If I was going to follow Jim anywhere, I'd be doing it alone and not with Dave.

CHAPTER 17

We went back to my house, and I made beef noodle soup and biscuits while Dave watched ESPN. I was putting the biscuits in the oven when I remembered Bonnie. I dialed her number and this time I got an answer.

"Bonnie, this is Annie Johnson," I said. "I know this is probably a bad time, but I wanted to ask you a quick question while I'm thinking of it."

"Yes?" she said in a suspicious voice.

"Did Danny ever see any other women while he was married to Donna, as far as you know of?"

I could hear her sigh. "No," she said. "Now if there's nothing more, I'm really very busy."

"I'm sorry," I said. "I know it must be really hard to take care of so many kids. Who do you get to watch them while you're at work?"

"My mother-in-law," she said. "Now if you don't mind, I really have to be going."

"I'm sorry to have bothered you," I said and hung up. I was a little annoyed by her attitude and I wasn't sure I understood it. Then again, maybe it was nothing more than her irritation over my suggesting that Danny might have been doing yet another unacceptable thing.

I called Donna next, after consulting with Dave. "Would it be possible for Dave and me to come and see you again tomorrow night?" I asked.

"What's the problem?" she said. "Did you find something out?"

"A few things, yes. I think you'll be very interested in one of them."

"Can't you tell me over the phone?" she said. She was starting to sound a little anxious.

"I think it would be better if we talked about it in person," I said, knowing I was making her all the more nervous.

"All right," she said. "How about seven o'clock?"

"That's fine," I said. "We'll see you tomorrow night."

*　　*　　*

When Donna opened the door for us the next night, I smelled liquor on her breath. She had trouble making eye contact with either of us as she said "Hello" and looked mostly at the floor. I decided to get right to the point.

"Donna," I said after we'd all sat down in her living room. "When Dave and I were at your mother's house, we found a sack of money in Danny's bedroom. It was a whole bunch of fifties and hundreds. There must have been several thousand dollars there. Do you know anything about it?"

Donna rose from her seat so quickly that it startled me. "Why that little . . . ." She clenched her teeth and her fists at the same time. "Where does he get off asking *me* for money when he had a stash like that?"

"So you didn't know about it?"

"No, I didn't know about it," she said. "Of course I didn't know about it. What do you take me for, an idiot?"

I sighed. "Do you have any idea where he might have gotten it?" I said.

She laughed. "How should I know?" she said. "Maybe he robbed a bank."

I wished I had a comfortable transition from my first topic to my second, but I didn't. "I know this is very personal," I said, "but we already know from Jim that you were aware that Danny was seeing other women while he was married to you."

She looked away and then down at the floor. "What about it?" she said in a defeated tone.

"Would you by any chance know if he was seeing anyone at the time he died?"

"Yeah, he was seeing someone," she said. "He was always seeing someone," she added with a sad little laugh. "He was doing it even before we got married."

I frowned. "Then why did you marry him?" I asked in a kind voice.

Donna shook her head. "I don't know. Because I'm crazy. Because I was in love. I loved him from the day I met him. I was only fourteen but I knew what love was all about. No one could tell me different. Everyone tried to tell me he was no good for me, even my friends, but I didn't care what they said. I loved him too much."

I gave her a sympathetic smile. "Do you know who he was seeing before he died?"

"No," she said. "I saw him with someone a few months back, but I'm sure he had a new one by the time he died. He never stayed with any of them long." She laughed. "That was my one consolation. I could always convince myself they never really meant anything to him because he wouldn't stick with them."

"How long did they usually last?" I said.

She swallowed hard. "They'd never lasted longer than a month," she said as her eyes started to glisten.

"Can you remember what she looked like?" I said. "The one you saw him with a few months ago?"

Donna sniffled. "Yeah, I sure can. She was real weird looking if you want the truth. She had long brown hair with this huge streak of gray down one side."

I looked at Dave and he frowned at me. I could see he didn't remember, but Donna had just described the woman we'd seen Danny with at La Casa.

"Where did you see them?" I asked.

"In our bed," she said, and her face turned pink.

"Do you know how we could find her?"

"I have no idea," Donna said. "I never even knew her name."

"Okay," I said. "That's really all we wanted to ask you." I got up to leave and so did Dave. "Oh, by the way," I added, "do you know who pays for Mrs. Patrinkis's housekeeper?"

Donna wrinkled her brow. "Her housekeeper?" she said with an astonished look. "I didn't even know she had one."

*   *   *

The next day, without telling Dave, I drove by Jim's garage and his apartment to see if I could find him. His car wasn't in sight at either place. I went back to the garage and back to his apartment again. Same result. I decided to go shopping. I got on I-76 going east and got off at Deptford. The Deptford Mall is large enough to satisfy my shopping addiction and it's rarely overcrowded. Unfortunately, that day Macy's was having a sale and I could barely get through the crowd. I stayed for about half an hour and left.

Then I tried looking for Jim again. I was in luck. He was at home. The problem was, I didn't know what to do next. I didn't want to talk to him. I only wanted to follow him. He'd never seen my car, but it was broad daylight, and he'd surely recognize me if he came out of his house.

It was then that I came up with my plan. I went home for my binoculars and hurried back, this time *without* a thermos of coffee. I'd learned that lesson on my first stakeout. His place was only two buildings from the corner so I parked on the street that intersected his. I could still see his building but I was reasonably sure he wouldn't spot me. I took out the binoculars (which I really didn't need because I was so close) and started spying on anyone I could find. If you haven't tried it, take it from me, it's fun for a while but generally it's just a big disappointment. Nothing really happens—or at least it didn't when I was doing the spying.

I spent three hours checking out Jim's apartment and those of his neighbors. By that time I was bored silly and nearly starving to death, so I hung it up for a while and went to McDonald's. By the time I got back, it was nearly four o'clock and starting to get dark. That was what I was really waiting for. Jim's car was still there and there were lights on in his apartment. I saw him walk past the window twice and the second time he looked out onto the street. I quickly slid down so that I was even with the dashboard. I kept telling myself he couldn't have seen me, but it made me nervous just the same.

At half past five, when it was almost fully dark, he

came out and got in his car, made a U-turn, and headed right for me. I could hardly believe it. I dove under the wheel, sure he'd seen me, but he drove right past. After several moments, I cautiously got up and looked behind me. He was nowhere in sight. There was a hill at the top of the first block, however, so I hoped I'd catch sight of him again once I got over it.

I turned my car around and sped up the street, over the hill, and through the first intersection. There was another hill at the end of the next block and I still couldn't see him. I sped down the second block and just barely spotted him three blocks down as he was making a right turn. I looked around for a squad car and when I didn't see one, I drove as fast as I could until I reached the corner where I'd seen him turn. He was only two blocks ahead of me then, and he was driving rather slowly, sort of cruising along as if he were looking for something or someone. I tried to keep a distance of two blocks between us and only sped up when he turned a corner or there was a hill to block my view. He went through neighborhood after neighborhood, occasionally slowing down even more than usual, until he circled one block three times. After that, he drove about five blocks to the east, parked his car, and started walking. I hadn't expected that and I wasn't sure what to do. I could hardly follow him at that pace without drawing attention to myself. So I decided to park a few blocks behind him and wait until he reached the end of a block. Then I moved a little farther and parked again.

Soon we were back at the block we'd circled. He turned the first corner, walked halfway down the block, looked around him several times, and casually stopped at a Honda parked along the curb. He went over to the driver's side, made some sort of movement near the door lock, entered the car, started it in less than a minute, and drove off. My eyebrows went up and I laughed without really meaning to. I was amazed that he'd done it that fast and even more amazed that I'd caught him doing it.

He drove the car at the speed limit until we were quite a ways away from where he'd taken it. I was so intent on following him that I wasn't really paying much attention to where we were going, which could have been a grave mistake if we hadn't ended up in a place so familiar to me.

He honked the horn when he arrived at his destination and a door opened. He drove the car inside and the door closed again. I shook my head. I couldn't believe what I was seeing. It just hadn't occurred to me that the chop shop would be there.

CHAPTER 18

About ten minutes later, Jim came out of the garage where he worked with three other men. I'd never seen any of the men that he worked with so I didn't recognize two of them, but the third was quite familiar. It was Chuck Dombrowski. I stared with my mouth open and wondered later why I was so surprised. Roger had told us that Chuck had been involved in the car thefts with Danny and Jim in high school. There was no reason to doubt that he could be doing it again just as Danny and Jim were.

I sat for a few moments trying to decide what to do next. My only sensible options were to go home or go to Dave's house and tell him what I'd seen. Going home was the safer of the two but I opted for seeing Dave. The truth was, I missed him and this was an excuse to see him.

When he answered the door, he stared at me and then smiled. "Hi," he said in a voice that showed his surprise.

"I've been trying to get ahold of you."

I took a deep breath and smiled. "Please don't get mad at me," I said with a wince.

He gave me a look.

"You have to promise first," I said.

He glared at me. "I'm not promising anything. If you don't want to tell me, then don't."

I pressed my lips together, walked into his living room, and sat down on the couch. Dave lives in a row house only a few miles from me. He has a maple tree out front, a newly painted deep-blue front door, red brick exterior, and three floors all to himself. He decorated the inside with modern, Danish-type furniture. It doesn't fit him at all and I'm dying to ask him what possessed him to furnish it that way, but I don't want to hurt his feelings.

"Chuck Dombrowski is involved in the chop shop thing with Jim," I said without meeting his eyes. When he didn't say anything, I looked at him. He was smiling and frowning at the same time.

"How do you know that?" he asked.

"They're running it out of the garage where Jim works," I said, avoiding his question for the time being.

Dave tightened his jaw. "You followed him, didn't you?"

I didn't answer.

He took the newspaper he'd been holding and slammed it down on an end table. "I told you not to follow him," he said. "You're starting to get stupid, Annie. You're taking too many chances. What happened to your common sense?"

I could feel tears coming on and I was determined not to let him see me cry. I didn't answer—again.

"Annie, look at me," he said. If I hadn't been so hurt, my anger would have taken over. I can't stand it when he talks to me that way. He has no right to tell me what to do and to treat me like I'm some kind of helpless, ignorant child. But I was afraid I'd be unable to stay calm, so I kept my mouth shut. I slowly raised my head and glared at him.

"How do you know about Chuck?" he said.

I waited several moments until I felt I could trust my voice and said, "I followed Jim and saw him steal a car. He drove it to the garage and a few minutes later, he and Chuck came out with two other guys."

"You're sure it was Chuck?"

"Positive," I said.

"How can you be so sure? It was dark, wasn't it?"

I sighed. "They were standing in the doorway and the lights were on inside. And I've seen him before and I recognized him. He has a very recognizable shape and I got a good look at his face."

"What about the other two? Did they look familiar?"

"No, I've never seen them before."

Dave nodded and put a thoughtful look on his face. "So we now know that Danny, Jim, and Chuck were involved in the car thefts," he said. Dave looked like he was thinking hard so I waited.

"I wonder what happened to the five thousand dollars Jim gave to Danny," he said. "And I wonder why he wasn't able to give him more."

I frowned. "Why do you think he should've been able to give him more?"

"Because of the business he was in. He has to be making out pretty big, wouldn't you think?" Then he frowned. "And so would Danny. He should've had a bit of extra cash of his own."

I shrugged. "I guess so. I don't really know anything about that sort of thing. It could be that the other guys make all the real money, and they only pay Jim and Danny a small percentage for every car they steal."

"Then why would they do it?" Dave said. "It isn't worth the risk, as far as I can see."

"Who knows?" I said. "Who knows why anyone does most of the things they do? I stopped trying to figure that out a long time ago."

Dave laughed. Then he suddenly looked serious again. "Let's think about this," he said. "It's a drive-by shooting, right?"

"Yeah?"

"And the money Jim gave him isn't on the body. Whoever did the shooting couldn't have taken it, though."

"True," I said. "But we can't assume he had it with him. He may have gotten rid of it already or just left it at home."

"The sack we found in his room," Dave said. "I wonder if that was it. We should've counted it when we had the chance."

I smiled. "Let's call Jim," I said. I walked into Dave's kitchen and picked up the phone. No answer.

"He's not home yet," I said. "Let's try the police instead."

Dave laughed. "Oh, yeah. Like they're going to tell you anything."

I dialed the police station and asked for the detective in charge of Danny's case. When I was told that he wasn't available, I asked if I could speak to someone else who was familiar with the file. The man transferred the call without another word.

"Detective Archer here," said another man in a deep, throaty voice.

I told him who I was and how Dave and I were involved. He'd known all about us since Dave had reported the money and the letters. I asked him if he could tell me the amount of money that was in the sack.

"Sorry, ma'am. I can't divulge that information."

"Can you tell me if it was five thousand dollars?"

He hesitated for just a moment before telling me once again that he couldn't divulge any information. The hesitation was enough of an answer for me.

"I think it was the money Jim gave him," I told Dave after I hung up. "And I think it was all there. He wouldn't tell me how much it was, but the guy hesitated when I asked if it was five thousand."

Dave grinned. "Good work, Detective Johnson. But where does that get us?"

"Well, at least we can be pretty sure where the money came from, so we can eliminate the theory about it being evidence of something else Danny was involved in."

"Let's call Roger," Dave said. "I want to ask him if Chuck ever asked him to get involved in the car theft business."

Dave got Roger's number from information since neither of us could remember it. Roger's wife answered and said Roger was tied up for the moment. Dave left his number and asked her to have him call as soon as he could.

"What's Jim's number?" Dave asked me as soon as he hung up.

I knew that one by heart (it was similar to mine) and

rattled it off. This time Jim was home.

"Jim, it's Dave Barrio," Dave said. "I have a couple of questions for you. First, did you give the five thousand to Danny in fifties and hundreds?"

After a moment, Dave turned to me and nodded.

"No reason," he said to Jim. "Next question. Did you have some sort of falling out with your mother?"

Dave looked at me and made a zipper-of-his-lips gesture to show that Jim wasn't answering. After a bit, Dave said, "I see. Okay, thanks. We'll be in touch."

"What did he say?" I said as soon as he hung up.

"The money was in fifties and hundreds, and he gets along wonderfully with his mother."

I made a face showing my disbelief. "My sentiments exactly," Dave said.

Just then, the phone rang and Dave picked it up. "Roger," he said. "Thanks for calling back. Just one quick question. Did Chuck ask you to come in on the car theft business with him?"

Dave paused while Roger answered. "We know Chuck's still doing it," Dave said. "Annie saw him with Jim at the garage where Jim works. It looks like that's where they're dismantling the cars." Another pause. "Okay, thanks," Dave said.

"He says Chuck never asked him either now or in high school," Dave told me after he hung up.

"I wonder why?" I said. "If Roger knew about it in high school, why wouldn't Chuck ask him to come in on it like he did with the package deal?"

"Maybe he didn't think the other guys would want him telling anyone else about the operation," Dave said.

"Well, that's true," I said. "Hey, I just thought of

something." I picked up the phone and dialed Jim's number. I wanted to see if Jim would give me the same story Roger had.

"Jim, it's Annie Johnson," I said. "I'm sorry to bother you again, but I have another question. Was Chuck Dombrowski involved in the car thefts with you and Danny back in high school?"

Total silence.

"Hello?" I said.

"What does that have to do with Danny's murder?" he said.

"Possibly nothing," I said. "Possibly everything. I just want to know."

Jim sighed and paused for another few moments. "Yeah, he was," he finally said. "Now get off my back."

"I followed you tonight," I said, and Dave punched me in the arm.

Total silence again. Then, almost half a minute later, he hung up.

"You idiot," Dave screamed at me. "What are you trying to do? Why would you tell him that? Don't you know he could be the killer?"

I stared at Dave. "He's his brother," I said. "There's no way he could have done it. But I think he might know who did. I was just hoping he'd tell me, that's all."

Dave's face and neck were bright red, almost purple. He ran his hand through his hair and started to pace the floor of his kitchen. When I sat down at the table and put my face in my hands, he left the room. I heard the television awhile later. I stayed where I was and tried to run what I knew through my mind. It was all so confusing. There were so many unanswered questions and things that just didn't make sense. I looked at my watch. It wasn't quite nine o'clock. I decided to call Bonnie.

I apologized for calling so late, and she was short but reasonably polite about it. "I wanted to ask you if Jim has had some sort of falling out with your mother," I said.

She sighed. "Well, I guess it depends on how you look at it," she said.

"What do you mean?" I asked.

"Jim has really tried over the years to stay close to her, he really has. But Ma has always claimed that Jim got Danny into trouble."

"You mean in high school?" I said.

"Then and even now," she said.

"Why does she blame him?"

"I thinks it's just because he's a year older. I know it sounds ridiculous, especially now, but that's how she's always felt."

"What does she blame him for now?"

"I'm not sure exactly," Bonnie said. "But she seems to even blame him for Danny's death. Now don't take that the wrong way," she hurried to add. "I don't mean that she thinks he killed Danny. I just think she feels that Jim got Danny involved with some shady characters and that's what got him killed. I told her she's wrong about all of it. I know Danny wasn't doing anything like that and Jim isn't either. I don't know who put such ideas in her head."

"Did your mother tell you what sort of trouble she thought Danny and Jim had gotten into?" I asked.

"No," Bonnie said. "She doesn't like to talk about it, although she's the one who always brings it up. I certainly never do. I don't believe it in the first place."

I shook my head. I couldn't understand Bonnie's total blindness where her brothers were concerned. "One more question," I said. "Do you know who pays for your mother's housekeeper?"

"Jim does," she said, "but my mother doesn't know it. He's been doing it for years."

"Thanks, Bonnie. You've been a big help."

I decided I needed to have another talk with Mrs. Patrinkis despite her physical condition. I had a feeling she might know more than she had told us.

CHAPTER 19

The next morning, I called Mrs. Patrinkis at 9:30. The housekeeper answered and brought the phone to Mrs. Patrinkis, who was lying on the couch. I forced myself to push away the guilt and asked her if I could stop by some time that morning for just a few minutes. She made a small whining sound when I asked, but after I told her it might help me find Danny's murderer, she said all right. Then I called Dave and asked if he wanted to come along.

"What do you want to talk to her about?" he asked.

"I want to get a better idea of how she feels about Jim," I said. "Bonnie seems to think she actually blames him for Danny's death, at least indirectly. I want to know why."

"Okay, I'll meet you there," he said.

I cleaned up the kitchen, had a second cup of tea, and drove to Mrs. Patrinkis's house. Dave was waiting for me when I got there. When he saw me, he motioned for me to get in his truck.

"Does she know I'm coming?" he said.

"No, but I'm sure she won't mind. You were there the last time and she obviously likes you. Besides, she asked both of us to solve the murder."

That seemed to satisfy him. We got out and knocked on the door. This time we only had to wait a few moments. The housekeeper came to the door and showed us to the living room where Mrs. Patrinkis was still lying on the couch. She had an afghan covering her up to her neck and the heat must have been turned up to ninety. Dave and I took off our coats and our sweaters and rolled up our sleeves. Mrs. Patrinkis barely stirred when we came in although the housekeeper announced that we were there.

I knelt on the floor near the couch where she could see me if she opened her eyes. "Are you feeling all right, Mrs. Patrinkis?" I said.

She moaned but kept her eyes closed. I motioned to Dave to come near me. "Go ask the housekeeper if she's sick and how long she's been like this," I whispered.

He nodded. A minute later he came back with the housekeeper. "She was like this when I got here this morning," the housekeeper said. "I made her a nice cup of tea and some toast but she didn't touch a thing." She shook her head. "I don't know what to do."

"I think we should call Jim," I said to both of them. I put my hand on her forehead. "She's burning up. I think we should take her to a doctor."

"I'll call him," the housekeeper said and she left the room. "He's on his way over," she said when she got back. "He says you can go now. He'll take care of everything."

Dave and I looked at each other. "That's all right," I said. "We don't mind. We'll stay with her until he gets here."

She started to object but I smiled and turned away so she left the room.

"Let's see if we can get her to talk," I whispered to Dave.

He gave me a disapproving look which made me feel awful. "Only if she's up to it," I added.

I put my hand on her forehead again and it felt warmer than ever. "Never mind," I said to Dave. "Do me a favor. Ask the housekeeper for a washcloth and dampen it with warm water."

When he came back, I placed the cloth on her forehead, and I saw one corner of her mouth turn up just the tiniest bit. I smiled. "I think she likes it," I said.

We stayed with her for the next fifteen minutes until Jim showed up. He looked a bit annoyed at seeing us there, but then he went straight for his mother.

"Ma?" he said. "It's Jimmy. I'm going to take you to the doctor."

The housekeeper entered the room and Jim asked her to get his mother's coat and hat. When she came back, the two of them helped Mrs. Patrinkis sit up and the housekeeper got her into her coat. Jim picked her up as if she weighed no more than a few ounces and carried her out the door.

I turned to the housekeeper. "I'm sure glad you were here," I said. "How many days a week are you with her?"

"Five since the week after Danny died. Jim asked me if I could double as a sort of companion to watch after her. He's afraid to leave her alone."

I smiled. "I would be too. I'm glad he's taking care of her. Does she know he's paying you to take care of her?"

The housekeeper shook her head. "No, he doesn't want her to know. I can't imagine why, but he insists I never tell her. Of course, she hasn't asked. I don't think it's occurred to her."

"Was he paying you when Danny was still alive?"

"Oh, yes," she said. "He hired me, oh, it must be five years ago now." She looked from me to Dave. "Would you like to sit down for a while? I just made a fresh pot of coffee."

"Sure, thanks," I said and we followed her into the kitchen.

"My name is Gretchen, by the way."

I introduced myself and Dave although I was pretty sure I'd done that before. We both took a seat at the kitchen table. She handed us each a cup of coffee and put a pitcher of cream and a bowl of sugar packets within our reach.

"By the way," I said when she sat down, "did Danny ask you not to clean his room when he was living here?"

Gretchen laughed. "Yes," she said. "He was quite insistent."

"Why hasn't it been cleaned since?" Dave said.

Gretchen stiffened slightly and then relaxed. "Because I was asked to leave it as it is," she said.

"Who asked you to do that?" I said.

"Mrs. Patrinkis. She doesn't want anything touched. I think she wants to preserve it as a sort of shrine. If she knew how filthy it was, she might reconsider, though."

"You mean she hasn't seen it?"

"Not as far as I know. She rarely goes upstairs. The steps have become too difficult for her."

"Then where does she sleep?" I asked.

"Usually I find her down here on the couch, just like I did this morning. I keep telling Jim we should get her a hospital bed for downstairs, but he says he doesn't want to make her feel like an invalid. I have to admit I do see his point."

I nodded. "Can I ask you a few questions about Danny?" I said. "I don't know if you know this, but Mrs. Patrinkis asked us to help find out who killed him, so you won't be doing anything she wouldn't approve of. In fact, I'm sure she'd appreciate it."

Gretchen shrugged. "Sure," she said. "Go ahead. I'll tell you what I can."

I thought for a moment. I hadn't planned on talking to Gretchen, so I hadn't thought about what I might ask her. But something suddenly came to mind. "Did he ever bring women home with him?"

She rolled her eyes. "He sure did," she said. "Wasn't a day in the week he didn't have someone in tow."

"Was it always a different one?" I asked.

"No, I think he had a few regulars but there were always the occasional stragglers. Don't get me wrong. It wasn't *really* every night of the week, but it was at least several nights a week."

"Was Donna ever here when he had a woman with him?"

She winced. "Yes, a couple of times. Donna came over wanting money or some such thing and she'd always come unannounced. I remember more than a few times when he had a woman here when she came."

"What happened? What did Donna do?"

"Screamed at him just like you'd expect."

"Did you ever hear her threaten him?" I said.

Gretchen gave me a surprised look. "No," she said as if that were unthinkable. "It was nothing like that, take my word."

"Okay," I said. "I understand." I pursed my lips. "Did anyone else ever come here and threaten Danny in any way?"

"Not as far as I know," Gretchen said. "I never saw anyone or heard anything like that. Far as I can recall, no one ever came here but Jim and Donna, and of course, the women friends he dragged home."

"Did Jim come to visit Danny," I said, "or just his mother?"

Gretchen shrugged. "Both, I'm sure. There were times Danny was out but when he was here, Jim talked to him too."

"Do you think they got along?" Dave said.

"Sure," she said. "Seemed like they did, anyway."

"How about Jim and his mother?" I said.

Gretchen frowned. "What do you mean?" she said.

"This will probably sound strange," I said. "It's confusing to me. But Bonnie told us that she thinks Mrs. Patrinkis and Jim had a falling out a long time ago and that it was because Mrs. Patrinkis always blamed Jim for the trouble that Danny got into, starting back in high school. She even thinks that Mrs. Patrinkis blames Jim for Danny's death."

Gretchen's eyes opened wide and she let out a gasp.

"Only indirectly, I mean. I don't think she actually thinks Jim killed Danny. The other thing is that Mrs. Patrinkis told us herself that the only one who ever took care of her was Danny and that she had no one left."

"She probably did see it that way," Gretchen said.

"Even though Jim was paying me, Mrs. Patrinkis never knew about it."

"But when we asked her why Jim couldn't help her now, she seemed so upset by just the mention of his name that she wouldn't even answer us."

"That was probably because of what Bonnie told you. She may have been thinking about that at the time."

"Then why do they seem to get along so well now?" I said.

Gretchen thought for a moment and shrugged. "Maybe he's convinced her she's wrong. He has been over here a lot more since Danny died. And now that I think about it, she didn't seem too happy to see him in the beginning. But it has started to change. She's started to ask about him now. She'll say to me in the morning, 'Do you think Jim's coming today?' I always have to say I don't know because I never know when he'll come. He doesn't make it every day. It's enough to break your heart."

I sighed and looked at Dave, then back at Gretchen. "Well, thanks Gretchen," I said. "You've been a big help. I'm glad we came."

She smiled and walked us out. "Stop by anytime," she said. "I'm only too happy to help. And I'm sure Mrs. Patrinkis would appreciate the company."

"I will," I said.

I'd be back sooner than I realized. That very same day, we solved the murder.

CHAPTER
20

Dave dropped me off at home after we left Mrs. Patrinkis's house. He had a carpentry job that he'd agreed to do himself and he was already late. I made myself a hard-boiled egg sandwich for lunch and followed it with two cups of tea. Then it was time to get down to business. If I didn't start thinking in an organized way, we were never going to solve the case, and so far I'd been anything but organized. I got a tablet of paper from my desk and started writing. I jotted down everything I could think of that we'd learned or that I had questions about. Then I made some phone calls.

Pam was home and Chuck was asleep, as I knew he would be. "I'd really like to ask Chuck this so I may call back later," I said, "but I'm too anxious to wait. Did Chuck say anything to you about selling the stolen merchandise from street carts in Philadelphia?"

"He sold some of it that way," she said. "Some things he sold in flea markets. Why do you ask?"

"I'm just trying to clear up a few loose ends," I said. "It's not that important."

I called Fred Maxwell next. It took his wife over a minute to convince him to talk to me, but he finally gave in. "What is it?" he asked in a flat tone.

"Didn't you tell me that you gave all the merchandise you took to Dan Albright, and then he sold it and gave you half the proceeds?"

"Yeah. That's the way he wanted it. It was his way of controlling things."

"So he probably did that with everyone who worked for him."

"I would assume so," Fred said.

"That's all I wanted to know," I said.

Next I called Roger. It was after ten so I was afraid he'd have left for work already, but I was lucky to catch him. "Roger, it's Annie Johnson," I said. "I wonder if you could help me with something."

"Anything," he said. "What can I do?"

"You followed Chuck and you saw him taking packages from Danny's route, right?"

"Correct."

"Are you sure it was Danny's route?"

"Of course, I'm sure," he said. "Danny gave me a map so I'd know where I was."

"Thanks, Roger," I said. "I'll keep in touch."

I called Pam back. "I know this is a lot to ask," I said, "but could you *please* wake Chuck up. This is a matter of life and death." (Being melodramatic gets them every time.)

"I can't do that," she said. (Well, almost every time.)

"I have to talk to him," I said in an urgent voice. "He's

the only person who can give me the information I need."

After a few more minutes of pressure she gave in. When Chuck answered the phone, he was groggy and not at all happy to hear from me.

"I'll try to make this fast," I said. "We talked to Dan Albright, who we know was running the operation, and to Fred Maxwell, who we know was working for him. According to Fred, Albright required him to turn over everything he took and then Albright would pay him half the proceeds after he sold it."

No answer.

"Why would he have made a different arrangement with you? Why were you selling your own merchandise in Philadelphia?"

Another few moments of silence. Then, "He probably didn't trust Maxwell to know how to get rid of the goods. You'd have to ask Albright."

"I already asked him about his arrangement with you," I said. "He said you weren't even working for him. Why do you suppose he'd say that?"

Silence again. There were definite advantages to questioning someone too sleepy to think quickly. "I don't know," he finally said. "I was working for him. I was stealing from Danny's route. I don't know why he said that."

"Did you know that Albright also asked Clint Farrow to join your little group?"

"What about it?" he said in a strained voice after yet another hesitation. "He could ask anyone he wants."

"When did he ask you?" I said.

"Uh, four, no—six months ago. I don't know. I can't remember."

"Thanks, Chuck," I said. "I'm sorry I woke you up."

I was just about to call Roger again when I got what Dave later referred to as one of my stupid but brilliant ideas. I drove to Chuck's house and waited, hoping he'd feel the need to have a conversation with whomever he was really working for, outside of Pam's hearing. I was there less than half an hour when he came out and got into his car, a dark green Chevy Impala from sometime in the late seventies. I waited until he was a block away and began to follow him. We ended up on I-76, went over the Ben Franklin Bridge and through the Philadelphia city streets until Chuck pulled alongside an American Delivery Company truck. He put on his flashers and went around to the driver's side. The driver didn't get out, however, so I couldn't see who it was and I couldn't risk getting any closer. After about five minutes of conversation, Chuck got back in his car and drove off. I decided to stay with the truck. I followed it to its next stop. The driver got out, took a package from the back of the truck, and delivered it to an upscale row house. On his way back to the truck, I got a good look at his face. It was Clint Farrow.

I decided to follow him for a while and see what happened. As you might guess, nothing happened, but I unknowingly gained some information that would be of great use to me only a short time later. I went home, made a few additions to my notes, and tried to call Dave. There was no answer on the cell phone in his truck so I left a message.

It was then that I remembered the maps. They were still in my purse where I'd put them the day we searched Danny's room. I pulled them out and studied the routes. It was the Philadelphia route that caught my attention. It included the area Clint had covered during the time I'd followed him that day.

What was Danny doing with a map of Clint's delivery

route? And why did Chuck find it so important to give up a day's sleep just to talk to Clint right after I'd questioned him about the package thefts? There had to be a connection. I tried calling Dave again and still got no answer. I left another message, this one a bit more urgent.

Then I got antsy, and when I get antsy, I get impulsive. I decided to check out all three of the other routes Danny had marked off and see if I recognized any of the drivers. I knew it might take me more than what was left of the day but at least I'd get a start on it. The three routes were all suburbs of Philadelphia, so it would take me close to an hour to get to one of them and even longer to the other two. I decided to try the farthest one first and work my way back.

When I reached Bolton Hills, it was only a little before noon so I had plenty of daylight left. I followed the route as quickly as I could, assuming the person who drove it had started several hours before I had. At 1:00 P.M. I saw the truck. I followed it for about an hour and saw nothing suspicious or unusual. I didn't know the driver and he didn't steal any packages. At 2:10, I left for the second of the three routes.

This one covered Bering Heights, another extremely wealthy suburb, just like the last one. It took me nearly an hour and a half to find that driver and I discovered right away that I didn't recognize him. I wanted to follow him anyway but I knew that if I did, I'd run out of daylight before I found the third truck, if I ever found it at all. I decided to abandon the second route and go to the third.

This was Wadesboro, a suburb just as plush as the other two, if not more so. It was almost four and getting dark when I finally spotted him. I was surprised at first, but then I told myself that it didn't necessarily mean anything. He was just driving a route, after all. It was his job and I knew that. I hadn't seen him do anything wrong and it was Clint who Chuck went to see, not him.

I was just about to go home when I saw him stop at a house, walk to the door without a package, and come back with one. I frowned and followed him another two miles. He did it again. And again. The houses he stopped at were dark and the neighboring houses were dark as well. He took only three packages over a ten-mile stretch and then he headed for home. I found the nearest phone booth and called Dave. This time he answered.

"You think he killed Art and Danny?" Dave said. "But why?"

"To cover up what he was doing. He hasn't been caught and neither has Clint."

"Then it could just as easily be Clint," Dave said.

"I don't think so," I said. "He was the one Danny went to, not Clint. He had good reason to worry that Danny would discover it was him. I don't know why Chuck confessed to stealing from Danny's route, though, unless he thought he was better off confessing to that than to stealing from the other ones. Maybe the operation they have going is a whole lot bigger than Dan Albright's was."

"But why would he kill Art?" Dave said.

"Art probably tried to help Danny find out who was threatening him and who set him up to take the blame for something he didn't do. He may have figured it out and confronted him, and then he killed Art to keep him quiet. He almost *had* to kill Danny after that. Even if Danny hadn't guessed who killed Art, he couldn't take any chances. He had no way of knowing if Danny already knew, and he knew that Danny was trying to find out. He probably figured he couldn't afford to take the chance of letting him stay alive."

"I think it's time to turn all this over to the police," Dave told me. "We can be pretty sure Roger killed Art and Danny, but we may get ourselves killed if we don't leave the rest of this to the cops."

I agreed. "I'll call Detective Archer and tell him we'll meet him at the station in half an hour. We can tell him and let him take over."

* * *

It turned out I was right about everything. When Dan Albright asked Clint Farrow to join his operation, Clint said no, just as he'd told us. But then he started his own, an even bigger and more profitable one. The first person he asked to join him was Chuck Dombrowski. The second was Roger Thornton, at Chuck's suggestion. Contrary to the story Roger had given us, Roger accepted. The greatest irony is that Roger was already a part of Dan Albright's group. He was the one stealing from Danny's route because he'd been too afraid to take from his own. So when Danny was accused of being a part of Dan Albright's group and came to Roger for help—not knowing, of course, that Roger was a member of the group—Roger became afraid of being caught himself. He knew Danny would continue to investigate the matter either until he believed he'd discovered the truth or until he actually had. So he turned Chuck in, thinking that the company and Danny would believe that the whole "gang" had been caught and abandon their investigation. That would protect Roger and Clint and they could continue their own activities, making sure not to take enough from any one area that it would become noticeable. In fact, that is how they'd always done it. Unlike Dan Albright's group, who took so many packages from each route that they were almost guaranteed to be caught, Clint's group took only a few from each route, spreading the thefts out over many areas. The ones marked on Danny's maps represented only a small percentage of the routes in Clint's scheme.

When Danny came to Roger for help, he told him that Art was helping too but that, so far, neither of them had been able to uncover anything. When Roger learned that no one but Danny was aware of Art's involvement, he decided to kill Art before anyone could make a connection. He also planned to kill Danny but thought he might get a bit of money from him first. Quite awhile after Roger sent the last of the letters, he phoned Danny and, in a disguised voice, arranged to have Danny drop off at a designated location as much money as he could raise by noon the next day. Danny didn't raise the money in time, however, because he wasn't able to get ahold of Jim until late the next night. Believing that his attempt to get money from Danny had been a waste of time, Roger killed him the day afterwards.

Danny, by the way, wasn't taking packages from anyone. He was innocent of that all along. And according to Jim, he got involved in the car thefts again just to help his mother. Dave doesn't seem to understand this but I think that's really sad. He was murdered for something he'd never been involved in and he did something illegal at great risk to his own well-being in order to help someone else. I know that doesn't justify what he did, but it does soften my feelings toward him just the same.